Kitty Valentine
Dates a Cowboy

Spin the wheel.

jillian dodd

JILLIAN DODD

Jillian Dodd, Inc.
Madeira Beach, FL
Jillian Dodd is a registered trademark of Jillian Dodd, Inc.

Editor: Jovana Shirley, Unforeseen Editing,
www.unforeseenediting.com

ISBN: 978-1-953071-17-0

Books by Jillian Dodd

London Prep
London Prep: Book One
London Prep: Book Two
London Prep: Book Three

The Keatyn Chronicles
Stalk Me
Kiss Me
Date Me
Love Me
Adore Me
Hate Me
Get Me
Fame
Power
Money
Sex
Love
Keatyn Unscripted
Aiden

Kitty Valentine Series
Kitty Valentine
dates a Billionaire
Kitty Valentine
dates a Doctor
Kitty Valentine
dates a Rockstar
Kitty Valentine
dates a Fireman
Kitty Valentine
dates an Actor
Kitty Valentine
dates a Best Man
Kitty Valentine
dates a Cowboy

That Boy Series
That Boy
That Wedding
That Baby
That Love
That Ring
That Summer

Spy Girl Series
The Prince
The Eagle
The Society
The Valiant
The Dauntless
The Phoenix
The Echelon

Love Series
Vegas Love
Broken Love
Fake Love

Girl off the Grid

Chapter One

"YOU NEED TIME off," my editor scolds.

"Are you kidding me, Maggie? I just returned from the islands."

"Kitty, I saw your posts, and I know it wasn't all fun and games. You haven't been the same since you got back. Do you realize you gave the heroine's best friend three different names over the course of this book?"

"Sure. I totally did that on purpose."

"Kitty …"

No, of course I didn't notice the problem with the names. And that isn't like me.

"I was just trying to keep you on your toes," I tease.

Normally, Maggie finds my sense of humor charming. At least, that's what I tell myself.

She is not so impressed this time around. "That's it. I'm putting my foot down. Frankly, I know I'm to blame for this."

"For what?"

"For driving you as hard as I've been. Granted, I don't call the shots, but I do have enough pull that I could stick up for you. You're not a machine. You are a person, and you're clearly in the midst of serious burnout."

My head snaps back so hard, it's amazing I don't give myself whiplash. "That's not true. I can handle it."

"Tell me the truth. When was the last time you showered?"

I am so proud of myself too. "This morning, thank you very much." I even sound smug when I say it, like I did some amazing thing by washing myself.

"Here's a better question. When you sent me this file with the three-named best friend, when was the last time you showered before then?"

"I would like to plead the Fifth," I grumble.

"I thought so."

"That's always the case. Ask any writer. When you're getting close to a deadline, you want everything to be perfect, and some things tend to fall by the wayside." Like bathing. Or brushing teeth. Or drinking anything but coffee and other caffeinated beverages.

"Regardless, you're slipping. This isn't criticism, trust me. It's concern. I've been with you since the beginning, and you aren't normally sloppy. You need some time off."

"Fine," I huff.

"Kitty, I'm just looking out for you. You've had a grueling schedule since we started with the tropes. As much as I want to keep you moving, I also know when to give you time to recharge. Now that the best-man book is finished, I want you to relax and enjoy yourself. Refresh and reset. We can talk in a few weeks."

"Okay, Maggie. I hear you loud and clear."

"Good. Now, maybe go find a man for fun."

"Right, like I could do that in two weeks."

"Anything is possible when you're young, Kitty."

"I'll see what I can do. Good-bye, Maggie."

"Bye, Kitty."

NEEDLESS TO SAY, I do not go look for a man. For two weeks, I mostly do things that I have been neglecting around the apartment. Now, here I sit on the rooftop, trying to soak up every last bit of sunshine and relaxation I possibly can.

The opening and closing of the roof door brings me out of my trance.

"I'm sure if your grandmother were here, she'd warn you about getting too much sun."

Matt stands over me, hands on his hips. I can't see much of him, even with my sunglasses on, thanks to the sun being behind him. But I can practically hear the smirk in his voice. I'm used to hearing it by now.

"I use plenty of sunscreen, thank you. And you're blocking the sun. Now, my tan is going to be uneven."

3

"Oh, the horror!" He crosses his hands over his chest and gasps.

"I know you can't see my eyes right now because of the glasses, but trust me, I'm rolling them."

He chuckles, going to the spot under the ledge where he stores his chair. "I needed a little fresh air. It's been a tough couple of days. The market's been volatile."

"So, that's why I keep hearing you muttering and cursing to yourself over there."

"You can hear that?"

"Every once in a while. You know, only when I'm trying to take a nap because I'm supposed to be recharging. It's no big deal."

"Recharging, or did you need naps after moving your furniture around at all hours of the night?"

"You heard that?" I ask sheepishly.

"Yeah, I heard that."

Oops. "Sorry, I didn't mean to wake you. I just decided on a whim that it would be fun to shake things up. Rearrange my furniture. Like they do on those house shows. It's amazing, all the design tips you can learn during a few weeks off. Maybe you need to take a little time off. I bet it would do wonders for you."

"Oh, sure. It's been doing wonders for you."

"And what is that supposed to mean?" I raise myself up on one elbow, pushing up my glasses and resting them in my hair.

He's stretched out in his chair, like always, his

bare feet practically in my face. I have to shove them away, and he snorts like the pesky big-brother figure he's turned into. "Let's start with the fact that you've rearranged your furniture at least twice in the past two weeks."

"What's so weird about that? I wanted a change. And that's the sort of thing people do when they have time off. All the little things they've been wanting to do but they were too busy."

"And how many times have you rearranged your books?"

"I do that all the time anyway!"

"And you finally opened up the jigsaw puzzle Hayley had gotten you for Christmas two years ago, which had been sitting in its box under the TV stand ever since. You told me so."

"Hey, that was a really cool present, and I felt like it deserved to be used."

Honestly, it's the coolest thing in the entire world. Hayley gathered hardcover versions of all of my books, arranged them, took a picture, and then had it made into a jigsaw puzzle.

"But you only put the border together. It's been sitting on the floor in the same place with the same amount of work put into it for two weeks."

"What is even the point of inviting you into my apartment when all you're going to do is criticize? And I'm sorry, but since when do you take notes on the things I do? You're starting to freak me out a little bit. Are you looking into taking up stalking as a second job?"

He shoots me a withering look.

"Or maybe private investigation?" I suggest.

"This is what friends do, Kitty. They point out when they feel like their friend is going off the deep end a little. I went in your kitchen yesterday to grab forks and saw you'd alphabetized your spice collection. I could eat off your kitchen floor; it's so squeaky clean."

"You're more than welcome to give it a try, if that's what you're into." I settle back down, pushing my sunglasses firmly back into place.

"I'm just trying to say, you're a workaholic."

"Gee, I had no idea."

"People like you and me, we can't handle having nothing to do. And, yes, we tend to burn out very easily. You should start running with me in the mornings. I find it helps me focus and clears my head."

"That's why I practice yoga. Don't tell me you didn't notice the rolled-up mat in the corner while you were so busy with investigating the jigsaw puzzle on the floor. And you'll notice, I've been eating a lot more vegetables and salads lately to make up for going off the deep end when I was on a deadline."

"Yeah, and look at all the good it's doing you— your yoga practice and salads. You're still wound up tighter than … I don't know what." He shrugs. "You're the writer. You have all the words."

I have more than a few words for him, come to think of it. "You know I don't like receiving unsolicited advice."

"Because you always take it as criticism. Sometimes, when people make observations, it's because they're genuinely concerned. News flash: people care about you."

I know he means it. And deep down, in the rational part of my brain, it means a lot to hear it. A writer's life is a lonely one. We tend to live in our own worlds, worlds we make up from scratch. We don't go to the office every day; there's nobody to monitor us.

If anything, Matt is the closest thing to a coworker I've ever had. I've been lucky enough to make a career of writing ever since college, so I never went through the whole nine-to-five schedule.

He's the one person I see almost every day. Sure, I visit Grandmother and Peter at least once a week, and Hayley and I see each other whenever she has time.

But that's it.

I have to take a deep breath and slowly let it out before responding. Crow has never been my favorite thing to eat, but it looks like I have a serving waiting for me. "Thank you," I manage. "I'm not used to having a lot of people in my life who genuinely care."

He's quiet for a minute.

JILLIAN DODD

I finally look up at him. "Well? Did I kill you?"

"Just about. You must've gotten too much sun if you're thanking me all of a sudden."

"Maybe I have, but that's not the point." I sit up, looking at him straight on. "Thank you. I'm trying to be a better person. More thoughtful, less argumentative."

"Oh. Don't change too much."

"Are you kidding?" I laugh. "I imagined you would jump up and click your heels."

"Well, you can keep imagining that, because it will never happen."

"You know what I mean."

He offers an actual, genuine smile. "Kitty, if I had such a problem with your argumentative attitude and your complete stubbornness, would I even talk to you anymore? Granted, having lunch or dinner in your apartment gives me a break from mine, but I could go just about anywhere. I like you the way you are. Mostly."

"You just had to slide that last word in there, didn't you?"

"Of course I did." He gives me a smug wink. "I mean, would you expect anything else?"

"Honestly, no. I know better by now." I roll onto my stomach to get a little sun on my back.

"Want some help?" When I look up at Matt, he's holding up his hands. "Sunscreen. It's not summer yet, but the sun will still burn you up. Especially since you're not, um, the outdoorsy type."

"Okay, but don't get handsy with me." I give him the bottle and settle my chin on my folded arms.

He snickers. "Right. Do you remember how we officially met?"

"What about it?"

"You threw up all over my rug—"

"Which I will replace! I keep telling you!"

"And then you stripped down to nothing and passed out in my bed. Now, I ask you, if I didn't get handsy with you that night, why would I do it now that I actually know you and know all the baggage you come with?"

"You are such a jerk!" I jump a little at the sensation of sunscreen hitting my back. "I don't have baggage."

"No, you're right. But you definitely have issues."

"Why do I even talk to you?"

"Because you find my sense of humor so endearing."

"Oh, a sense of humor? That's what you call it?"

I would keep going, but there's a problem brewing. A problem caused by the hands now sliding over my back, my shoulders, the back of my neck.

Here's the thing.

Matt's seriously hot. Like, breathtakingly hot. Back in the day, before that whole unfortunate *getting drunk and puking and stripping* incident, I was too intimidated by his looks to even talk to him. For an entire year in fact.

That hotness hasn't changed. If anything, it's like he gets better-looking all the time. It's so unfair that men age well. Not that he's old. But time shouldn't work its magic on him like it does.

"Would you relax?" He digs his thumbs into my shoulders while rubbing the lotion in. "God, you're a mass of knots."

Yeah, because I don't know what to do with the weird, fluttery feeling he's giving me.

I seriously need to get a grip on myself. This is Matt. My annoying neighbor from across the hall, who I wouldn't love nearly as much if it wasn't for his adorable dog. So what if he happens to be scorchingly hot? The funny thing is, I used to get so nervous around him that I never uttered a word to him.

I honestly haven't thought much about his hotness in a long time. Now that I've gotten to know him better, his sarcasm and unceasing devotion to knocking me down a peg or two have superseded the effect his looks have on me.

But right now? With his rather large, rather strong hands rubbing sunscreen into my skin?

It's all I can think about. And things are about to get worse if he doesn't stop.

"Thanks. I think I'm okay." I scramble up to my hands and knees and then stand on shaky legs. "Actually, I think I should head inside. I've been out here for way too long. I feel a little woozy."

He rubs his hands together, like he's getting rid of the rest of the lotion on his palms.

Is he grinning? Why is he grinning? Dear Lord, does he think he turned me on just now?

Would he be entirely wrong if he did think that?

"Drink a lot of water," he advises. "Rest. Keep yourself cool. You do look awfully flushed and worked up."

"Sure, sure. Will do." I can't even look at him. It would be like getting heated up over my brother or a cousin or something. It's gross.

Matt's the last person in the world I need to be crushing on. He is only good for sharing takeout with and occasionally venting to when things in my life go south.

Besides, as soon as I get back to work, it'll mean getting back to dating my next trope. I haven't figured out who I'll be writing about yet, but something tells me a few rounds of hot and heavy action, just like I had with Kellen, will set me back on the right track.

Because the last thing I need in my life is a crush on Matt. He would never let me live it down. I would have to move or something, and the very thought of that makes my stomach turn. But I would still rather put up with packing and moving and settling in someplace else than with the possibility of dying from embarrassment every time our paths cross.

Chapter Two

"SO, HOW DO you feel about starting work again?"

I can tell Hayley the truth. I don't feel like I have to put on any fake confidence with her. "God, I can't wait. I've been going nuts with nothing to do."

"I thought you were working on the jigsaw puzzle!"

I glance over to where the puzzle waits. Matt wasn't kidding around or exaggerating. I've only filled in the borders. "Of course, I love the puzzle. It's not the puzzle's fault I've had the attention span of a gnat lately. I blame the internet."

"I'm only teasing." Hayley flashes one of her winning smiles, which is just as dazzling on my phone screen as it is in real life. "You need more than a jigsaw puzzle. You need a bigger life in general. But you knew that already."

"My life is big in general! Can I achieve balance? I mean, I could try. But you have this way of making it sound like I'm the only person in the world who has ever failed to achieve work-life balance. And that just isn't true." I narrow my eyes at her. "Besides, don't even pretend like you aren't a workhorse."

"I need to be if I ever want to make partner." My best friend is a driven girl, and I have to give her credit for working hard toward her goals.

"But you know what I mean. You took calls, and I even saw you sneaking in work emails when we were away for your sister's wedding."

"Like I really wanted to do that! And it's not like I was initiating. I was replying to emails from other people."

"I know. I know. Look what it got you. A promotion to junior associate."

"Exactly. You're right though; we both work a lot. But you are practically a hermit. At least I'm around other people. Anyway, anyway"—she waves a hand around in front of the screen—"I didn't call to argue with you."

"Well, that's good to hear." I plop down on the couch, pulling my feet up under me. "So, what's up?"

"You know what time it is." Slowly, she raises the spinner, so I can see it.

"Are you sure you didn't rig it this time?"

Last time we spun to see which romantic hero I would write about and therefore date, she'd changed every entry to Best Man, determined to hook me up with the best man at her sister's wedding.

Kellen. He was hot and definitely knew what he was doing. That part of things went well. Extremely well actually. We were very compatible.

It was the whole drama after coming home that put an end to things. Namely the fact that he'd lied to me about his gambling addiction. These past few weeks, I've wondered if he's the reason I was thrown off. It was difficult to end my book with a happy ending, knowing we hadn't really gotten one.

I wish him well, and from what I understand, he's working hard to turn things around.

And it's time for me to move on. If only because I need to start writing another book soon.

And because, let's face it, if Matt's getting under my skin, I need to get laid.

"I didn't rig it, I promise. Look." She spins it once and then again. The first time, it lands on Biker—as in motorcycles—and the next time, Chef.

I snap my fingers and pout. "Darn it. I could go for a sexy scene on top of a prep table."

"Who knows? Maybe we'll land on it again."

We do not land on it again.

What we do land on, however, makes my eyebrows just about shoot up off my head. "Oh, hello."

Hayley giggles. "Cowboy! Giddyup, little lady!"

"Gee, what a terrible job I have." I pretend to sigh and swoon.

"Listen, if you're not up to the challenge, I would be happy to do this for you and tell you about it after our dates."

"Oh, you're such a sweet friend. Do I tell you

that often enough?"

"It's okay. I don't do it for the recognition."

Once I finish laughing, I shake my head. "Sorry. For this one, my research has to be firsthand. I'll catch you up on how things go."

"You know I'll be waiting."

"Now, the ever-looming question: where will I find this guy? It was one thing when I knew where to find a best man, you know?"

"You need help? I'll find you a cowboy."

"I love your confidence, but where the heck would you find a cowboy?"

"I have my ways." When I roll my eyes, she sticks her tongue out at me. "We have all kinds of clients, remember?"

"Last time you hooked me up with one of your firm's clients, it didn't go so well."

She grimaces at the memory. My brief fling with a rock star—a has-been, if I'm being honest—didn't exactly end well. "We'll do better this time. Let's see … cowboys. That makes me think of ranchers and oil tycoons."

"Tycoons. That sounds like the sort of client your firm would handle."

"I'll see what I can do. Maybe ask your grandmother if she knows anybody in the oil business too."

I wrinkle my nose. "No, thank you. I'm not trying to date somebody who's decrepit."

"Decrepit, old men with money generally have

young grandsons, who are prepared to inherit that money," she points out with a sly wink.

"Why, Hayley"—I clutch my invisible pearls—"you sound downright mercenary."

"Just saying. I'll take a look at some of our client lists and find out if there's anybody coming into town anytime soon. I'm sure we can find someone."

"*We* don't have to do anything, you know. I don't want you to feel like you have to spend your valuable time working on this."

"It's a diversion. I mean, look what I would be doing otherwise." She pans the phone's camera, letting me see the piles of folders and stacks of paper spread out over her coffee table and the floor surrounding it.

The girl has a way of making me love my job more than I already did. "Is there anything I can do for you? Maybe order you up some dinner or a case of wine or something?"

"The case of wine sounds pretty good right about now," she admits. "I'm going to try to take a little time off this weekend. Do you want to catch brunch?"

"Yes!"

"Is that enthusiasm for me or for brunch?"

I wince, squinting my eyes until they're almost shut. "Both?"

"Honestly, that's better than I expected."

✧　✧　✧

"THE OIL BUSINESS?" Grandmother looks beyond me, over at the wall behind where I'm sitting in her parlor. "Hmm. Do I know anyone …"

"What's this about?" Peter joins us with a pot of tea.

No matter how many times Grandmother reminds him he doesn't need to act like a paid servant anymore—she's hired help to replace him now that they're together as a couple—old habits die hard. He's used to taking care of her, seeing to her needs. I guess when things have been a certain way for more than thirty years, it'll take more than a few months to change it up.

"My new book hero has to be a cowboy," I explain while he pours for the three of us.

He gives me a wink. "I didn't know you rode."

"I'm sure I could learn."

"The only people I've ever known who made their living in oil are long dead," Grandmother confesses with a shrug.

I can't wait to tell Hayley I was right, no matter how immature it makes me. It probably shouldn't have been my first thought, but a girl has to take her victories someplace, and Hayley is a super genius who's almost never wrong about anything.

"I figured it was worth asking." I pick out an egg salad sandwich with the crusts cut off. "Is this your egg salad recipe?" I ask Peter.

"Of course. I know better than to try to serve you someone else's recipe."

So, maybe Grandmother isn't the only person he likes to do little things for.

"You know"—Grandmother places her cup and saucer on the table between us with a thoughtful expression—"I am chairing a charity ball, scheduled to take place this weekend. It's for the Children's Hospital. There are bound to be a few heavy hitters there."

Why does Peter look so relieved?

"That's a good idea. She could go with you."

She turns to him with a frown. "My, it didn't take long for you to arrive at that conclusion."

Whoops. Something tells me there's been trouble in paradise, and I walked right into it.

I take a second sandwich just for the sake of having something to do. Good thing they're so yummy.

"Don't be offended." He pats her hand with a gentle smile. "But we've had this discussion. It would be better for you if someone other than myself attended the ball with you."

Oh, of course. Yet another issue that won't magically go away. The fact that Grandmother has already cut people out of her life for being anything less than thrilled when they found out she and Peter started a relationship. I can only hope I'm as kick-ass as she is someday.

And I very much wish I'd been there when she told off her number one frenemy, Whitney.

I clear my throat. "I'm always up for a ball."

This is a lie. I don't love going to these fancy-schmancy events. Usually wondering in the back of my mind how long it'll take before I do something awkward.

Not if do. *When* I do. It's pretty much inevitable.

If it gets Peter off the hook though, I'll gladly go. Not only has he taken care of her all these years, but he's also made her so happy since they got together after her heart attack a few months ago. Life events like a heart attack tend to put things into perspective and show us what we otherwise were missing.

Plus, I do need to find a cowboy. Hayley made a good point. Wealthy, old men generally have wealthy grandsons, and it's the grandsons I'm interested in.

Grandmother seems to shake herself a little before turning to me, like she forgot I was here. Too busy staring daggers at her boyfriend. "Well, dear, since it would appear I'm suddenly going solo, I would love to have you there. And even if we don't land you an oil magnate, there are bound to be scads of wealthy, young men there."

I glance at Peter. "Hey, it doesn't matter if they're wealthy. I don't care about that."

Like he needs to hear her going on about money right now. Sometimes, she just doesn't think. I love her to pieces, but she's not always sensitive to how her comments might be taken.

It strikes me—and not for the first time—that Peter has to be a brave man. It's one thing for him to deal with her social circle being a bunch of snobs, but then he has to deal with her, and that can't be a walk in the park.

At least he's used to her ways. He wouldn't love her if he wasn't.

Why does that immediately bring Matt to mind?

"Oh dear."

Thank goodness my grandmother figures out a way to change the subject because, now, I don't know what the heck sort of tricks my brain is trying to pull on me. Making me think of Matt just because he said he liked me the way I was.

I mean, why wouldn't he? I'm a freaking treat.

"What is it?" I ask.

"I nearly forgot. There's something else I wanted to discuss with you."

When her blue eyes slide over toward Peter and they share a slight grin, I don't know whether to be glad for the change of subject or regretful. They're plotting something.

"I'm afraid to ask … what is it?"

"You might or might not recall, but there's a special day coming at the end of this month …" Her grin turns to a smile.

"Oh jeez." I blow out a long sigh, looking up at the ceiling. "You know I don't go for the big, fancy gestures, Grandmother. I don't need anything special."

"But you deserve it, which is another issue entirely."

"Can I talk you out of wanting to plan something?"

Peter chuckles. "Talk your grandmother out of wanting to plan something? Why not talk the sun out of the sky while you're at it?"

Grandmother lets him know how she feels about this with a single sniff before tossing her head. "Fine. If you would rather everyone ignore your birthday this year, that's just wonderful."

"I didn't say—"

"Just because it means a great deal to see my granddaughter happy."

"You don't have to cancel every—"

She heaves a sigh I would laugh at if she wasn't using it against me. "Don't worry about me, dear. I wouldn't want you to feel obligated to your grandmother simply because there's no telling how many of your birthdays I'll live to see."

My jaw's on the floor by the time she turns to Peter.

"I think I need to go upstairs and lie down."

"You're strong as an ox, and you know it." He laughs, though he does stand to help her to her feet.

I'm getting my things together when he joins me in the front hall.

He runs a hand over his head and what little gray hair is left. "She really is something."

"Yeah, she is." I look up the stairs. "And super subtle."

"You can't be too hard on her. She likes to have

her way, yes. But in this case, she wants to do something nice for you because she loves you."

"Which is the only reason I didn't flat-out refuse. But her idea of a good time and mine are totally different. I don't want one of those swanky parties. I want to feel like I can breathe and be myself without dozens of pairs of eyes staring at me and judging me."

He slides his hands into the pockets of his slacks. "That much we agree on."

Yes, we would, wouldn't we?

"Can you talk some sense into her? I'd like to go to dinner at a quiet place, just us, than do anything else."

"I'll see what I can do. Now, maybe you can do something for me." He looks up the stairs this time with a rueful smile. "I know she wants to battle any dragon who comes her way, standing in front of me with a sword and shield. I would rather she not."

"She does it because she loves you."

"Now, don't use my words on me." But there's a twinkle in his eye. "And I want to avoid uncomfortable situations whenever possible because I love her. Between you and me, one thing a domestic servant knows is the way people talk. Those who are good at their job know how to fade into the background. Some employers and their friends completely lose track of who occupies a room with them. They say whatever is on their mind about who and whatever is the current topic of interest."

The twinkle fades, and his face falls a little. "They say terrible things. I wouldn't have them talking about her that way."

I lean in and kiss his wrinkled cheek. "You're the one with the sword and shield, and don't think I don't know it. I wasn't kidding all those times I said you were my favorite thing about her. There's no contest."

"You'll explain things to her and look out for her at the ball?"

"I sure will."

And if anyone there thinks they can get away with gossiping about either of them, they'll get an earful from me.

Chapter Three

"SIT UP STRAIGHT, dear."

Grandmother is feeling extra cranky tonight. Awesome. I'm so glad we're spending time together in her car, stuck in traffic on the way to the ball.

So she can criticize me.

"You should wear your hair down more often," she admonishes. "Swept over one shoulder in that strapless dress? Now, that would be dramatic. That would be eye-catching."

I touch a self-conscious hand to the updo I spent an hour on. "I'm sorry I didn't run my choice of hairstyle past you but last time I got dressed up, you told me to show off my shoulders."

"Don't get snippy with me."

"I wasn't trying to." *I was.* "You're so grumpy tonight."

"I've worked my fingers to the bone for this event, and I want to be certain it goes well." She checks out her lipstick in a gold compact before touching up the powder on her nose. "Last year, Whitney chaired. I want to outdo her in every way, if you must know."

"Obviously. But I'm sure it'll be great. You always know how to make things perfect."

She snaps the compact shut with a decisive click. "I wish that were true."

There's a touch of sadness in her voice, and immediately, I soften under it.

"Are you thinking about Peter?"

"Who else?" She turns her face to mine, and I hate the strain there. "I wish he were here with me. Not that I mean to offend you, dear."

"I don't take offense. I'm sure you would rather have the person who means more to you than anybody right here by your side."

"I wish he understood better how little I care what they think. What any of them think."

"I know you don't care, but he cares about you, and he wants to avoid putting you in a situation where things will be uncomfortable and tense. Considering you're about to show that Whitney up tonight and teach her how a charity function should be run, no wonder he wanted to take himself out of the equation. He wanted to step aside, so everything would be perfect for you."

"I didn't want him to. What's the good of perfection if you don't have the person you love with you?"

We're not generally the touchy-feely type together, but we've been more so since her heart attack. She was most definitely raised before that became a thing.

25

I reach over and pat her hand. "Sometimes, when people love us, they think they know better about what we need than we do. I think that might be the case here. He's so sure he's going to hold you back, and that's the last thing he'd ever want to do." I lean in, whispering, "And he knows how stubborn you are. Even if your relationship hurt you somehow, he knows you'd insist it doesn't."

Her crimson lips come together in a thin line.

"I thought so." I pat her hand one more time before looking out the window to gauge where we are. "I think we're getting closer. Should be there any minute."

"I'm sure they've destroyed everything by now," she frets.

I don't know who *they* are, but I feel sorry for them if even one centerpiece is a millimeter out of place.

It isn't. None of them are. The ballroom is magnificent, like something out of a dream. Candlelight, crystal, dramatic lighting, and so many flowers. The scent of roses and peonies hangs in the air. They drip from the elevated centerpieces and from an elaborate arch set above the doors leading into the room.

I accept a glass of champagne from a silver tray and breathe a sigh of relief. She seems pleased, and I spoke up for Peter, like I'd promised. Now, all that's left is not embarrassing Grandmother in any way—and, oh yes, finding a cowboy.

No biggie, right?

"Kathryn, dear." Grandmother grabs me in passing and pulls me in close. "The very tall man wearing a cowboy hat in the middle of a charity ball is Patrick Cleary, CEO of Cleary Oil."

I can't miss the man in the cowboy hat. Not only does he tower over almost everybody else in the room, but also, you know, he's wearing a freaking cowboy hat with a tuxedo.

He's also at least sixty years old.

My heart sinks. "Does he have sons?"

"From what I remember, yes, he does." She pats my cheek with a distracted hand, already looking over my shoulder at somebody or something that needs attention. "He might've brought them with him, but I don't know. There were several last-minute additions to the guest list."

There are maybe three hundred people here at the moment, but Patrick Cleary's voice booms out over the low roar of conversation and laughter. I circle the group of people he's standing in the center of and observe him. Black-and-silver hair stick out from under his hat, and he has dark eyes with deep laugh lines at the corners.

Okay, so he seems like a fun guy. The people around him laugh genuinely at the story he's telling.

Are any of them his sons?

Jeez Louise, I'm no better than a gold digger. Stalking him in case he brought his rich sons along.

"She did a good job with this, I guess."

My shoulders tense at the comment. Patrick Cleary might as well not exist at the moment since somebody's talking about my grandmother.

Maybe it's the Brooklyn in me, or maybe it's the fact that I have no other family to defend, but the snotty tone in whoever's voice I just heard has me ready to fight.

I glance around until the owner of that snotty voice reveals herself. Tall and willowy with her hair down and pinned to the side to flow over her shoulder. She's chatting with a couple of other girls and wearing a snide smirk.

"Granted," she continues, "my aunt's work last year raised an unprecedented amount of money for the hospital. I'm sure good old Cecile had more than enough on her hands, teaching her boyfriend how to act in public. No wonder he isn't here tonight. He'd probably wander around, picking up empty glasses and clearing plates from the tables."

What's that feeling in my head? Like somebody kicked a beehive over. There's a buzzing in there now. It's almost deafening.

"Excuse me." I take a few steps toward their cluster.

She turns my way. "Yes?"

I'd guess she's roughly my age, maybe a little older. It strikes me as sad that somebody so young could be so close-minded.

"I was just wondering exactly who you think

you are, talking about Peter that way. Do you even know him?"

She sniffs, looking me up and down. "Do you?"

"I do in fact. He's my grandmother's companion."

Boom. Big, bright red spots pop up on her cheeks like magic. Not that she'll back down that easily. "Oh, is he? That would make you the writer, wouldn't it?"

"I'm her only grandchild, so yes."

"You write that trashy stuff, don't you?"

"Trashy?" I fold my arms but otherwise stay perfectly still.

"Romance." She wrinkles her nose. "I can't imagine that takes much work. It must be nice, knowing there's a safety net in place once you decide to stop writing filth."

"You have no idea what you're talking about. Not only is romance not the same as filth, but there's also a place for both." I take a step closer. "As for knowing there's a safety net in place, don't even get me started. Or did you somehow earn the trust your grandparents had set up for you before you were even born?"

That's a guess, but knowing Whitney is her aunt tells me it's a pretty good guess.

Her eyes narrow a second before her mouth opens like she's about to come up with something really, truly nasty.

Which is when a knight comes in and saves the

day. "Hi, honey." Suddenly, there's an arm around my waist, and a tall, firm man in a tuxedo is leading me away, toward the bar.

"Wha—who—"

"Just relax."

Whoever he is, he's strong. And fast. Before I know it, we're practically on the other side of the room.

"What are you doing?" I finally manage to catch my breath long enough to speak, and then I plant my feet once we've put a little space between us and that wretched girl.

"Avoiding a catfight, right here in the middle of the Children's Hospital fundraiser."

I realize he's laughing a split second before I glance up at him. I practically have to crane my neck, the man towers over me.

And he's extremely handsome.

Other things matter more right now though.

"Thanks a lot, but I can handle myself." I side-step him, so I can get another look at that witch whose extensions I'm about to tear out.

He sidesteps, too, blocking me. "I've seen you walking around with the kind lady chairing this ball, and I don't think she'd like it much if she knew you were throwing fists."

"I have no intention of throwing fists. I can't claw her eyes out with my fists clenched."

She's in the same spot, saying something snippy to her friends and looking over her shoulder at us.

The skank.

He laughs again. "Come on. Let me get you a drink. You deserve one after dealing with that." He ushers me to the bar.

"She has no right to talk about them."

"And I'm afraid you're going to crack a tooth if you clench your jaw any tighter. What would you like to drink?"

"Bourbon."

"Got it." He requests our drinks from the girl behind the bar, and soon, he presses a glass into my hand.

"Thank you," I say before taking a big gulp of the amber liquid.

I probably shouldn't drink it so fast, but he's right—whoever he is.

"So, who was she talking about?" When I glance up, he shrugs. "You said she has no right to talk about them like that. Who was she talking about?"

"My grandmother and her partner, Peter. He's the best. He's like a grandfather to me."

"That's nice."

"He used to be my grandmother's butler." I look up to check his reaction.

Dark brows draw together over a straight nose. "I see."

"So, I guess you think that's ridiculous too?"

He holds up his free hand. "Now, miss, I never said that. I'm not one of those highfalutin snobs like her." Then, he slides a finger under his collar like he's uncomfortable. "I hate these events. My daddy insisted I come with him since we're in town this week and my mama was always a big supporter of children's hospitals and programs for the families of sick kids. She's gone now, but I think it would've made her happy to know we're doing our small part."

"I'm sorry you lost your mom."

"Me too." He offers a tight smile. "Anyway, here I am. Forcing a smile for a bunch of people I'll never see again."

I hold out a hand. "You also saved that girl's life back there because I would've killed her. Kitty Valentine."

"That's quite a name." His handshake is firm, his hand big enough to swallow mine. "Paxton Cleary."

Bingo.

Do my eyes widen just a little too much when he says it? I try my darnedest not to look too happy at having accidentally attracted just the man I was looking for. "It's nice to meet you. You're a lifesaver."

"It was the perfect excuse to steal you away and pull you over here." He looks me over with his coffee-colored eyes, and his smile widens.

Bingo again. He's interested. This is going well. *Don't mess this up, Kitty.*

"So, what do you do for fun, Paxton Cleary?" I toss my head a little because, well, that's how people flirt. I'm trying to flirt. I'm trying to make him think I'm not a low-class troublemaker too.

He purses his generous mouth. "Hmm. I enjoy football, though in Texas, you either enjoy football or you're shunned by friends and family, so I didn't have much choice in the matter. I enjoy movies. Old ones in particular."

"Me too!"

"Favorite director?"

"Billy Wilder."

A smile lights up his face. "Me too! Elia Kazan is a close second."

"Good choice."

Just the fact that he can name-drop like that tells me he knows a little something.

"You have good taste."

"I like to think so."

He looks me up and down again in a way that makes my cheeks flush.

His glass is empty, and he signals the bartender for a refill. Just as she's about to pour a fresh drink, Paxton is hit from behind and lurches forward, causing her to splash his tuxedo sleeve with alcohol. As the bartender apologizes and tries to wipe off his sleeve, a busty blonde clings to Paxton's arm.

"I am so sorry!" she gasps. "I don't know what's wrong with me. I guess I stumbled."

Right. She stumbled and just happened to fall against him.

I do my best to keep a straight face.

"Oh!" The supposedly clumsy girl feels up Paxton's arm. "Did I ruin your tuxedo? I'm so, so sorry."

"No you didn't. These things happen," Paxton tells Busty while easily pulling his arm out of her grasp before turning his attention to the bartender. "It's not ruined. Don't worry about it a bit," he assures the girl who looks close to tears.

Meanwhile, here I am. Standing here like an idiot, watching this unfold. Wondering how there's even a universe where this girl thinks she's not painfully obvious.

To everybody but Paxton anyway. He's too busy making sure the bartender knows she's not going to lose her job over this. The woman waits, smiling a smile that doesn't quite reach her eyes.

I'd chat with her if she'd acknowledge my presence. She only has eyes for Paxton though. When he doesn't immediately return her attention, she rolls her eyes and walks away.

"Oh, you just keep on rolling," I whisper before taking a sip of my drink.

"Hmm?" Paxton turns his attention back to me. "What'd you say?"

"Nothing. You okay?"

"Sure. Just a little vodka. I might have to spill a dash of olive brine on there to make it a dirty-martini situation. Though I've always been more of a whiskey man."

"I enjoy whiskey myself, as you know." I raise

my glass to him. He touches the rim of his glass against it.

"What did we toast to?" he asks with an honest-to-God twinkle in his eye, leaning in so I can smell his intoxicating cologne.

What did we toast to? Oh, I can think of many things.

Chapter Four

"SO, WHAT HAPPENED next?"

I shrug and then take a sip of my Bloody Mary. "Nothing much. His dad was looking for him, so he had to go. But he did ask me to dinner tonight, and of course, I said yes. I gave him my address, and he'll be there later to pick me up."

Hayley sits back in wonder, shaking her head. "How you manage to find men so easily, I have no idea."

"Easily? Did any part of what I just described sound easy? I was about two seconds away from clawing somebody's eyes out."

"But I mean, it just so happened he was exactly who you were looking for."

"That's true. I guess I got lucky again. Though honestly, considering that he saved me from ruining my grandmother's reputation forever, I'm a little more grateful for that part than I am for meeting a rich cowboy."

"What's his name again?"

"Paxton Cleary."

She whips out her phone and types the name in

while I nurse my drink. That bourbon definitely went down too quickly last night. I should've paced myself, if only for Grandmother's sake, but I was so steamed when we first got to the bar.

I'm still steamed in fact. If that wretched thing were in front of me right now, outside of a fancy ball chaired by my grandmother and surrounded by people who know her, it would be a whole different story.

I know when Hayley's jaw pretty much hits the table that she's found Paxton's picture. "Oh, holy hell. He's too hot. It's burning my eyes."

I'm giggling as I take the phone from her to check out what she found. Is it just me, or are my panties ready to melt off?

Because as hot as he was in a tuxedo, he is about a million times hotter than the sun when he's dressed in jeans, cowboy boots, a flannel shirt, and a Stetson hat. In one picture, he's sitting astride a gorgeous chestnut horse. In another, he's grooming a horse in the stables, looking over his shoulder to grin at the photographer and showing off a butt that looks like a denim-covered peach.

There goes my jaw too. "I'm dying. I literally can't breathe."

"And you're going to dinner with him tonight?"

"Great. I wasn't already nervous enough. Now, I just know I'm going to say something dumb because I'm not going to be able to stop thinking about these pictures."

"You can blame it on me. Tell him your best friend stalked him online and found this photo shoot for *Forbes* and it's basically soft-core porn."

I can't stop laughing even though I'm blushing to the roots of my hair. It's like having a sunburn. "You're just making it worse!"

"All I have to say is, if this next book doesn't burst into flames in my hands from the hotness inside, I'm going to have your hormone levels tested."

"He's probably the best-looking of all of the guys I've dated. What do you think?"

"Oh, without a doubt. He's even hotter than Dr. Jake."

"Do you stalk all of my dates online?"

"Don't you know by now that your life is one endless distraction for me? If it wasn't for you, I would have to actually work through the road-blocks I face rather than pretend they don't exist." She taps her screen, nodding. "He's easily the hottest. And the way you make it sound, he's a really nice guy too."

"Honestly, if I had met him on the street, I wouldn't have known who he was. He had this really easygoing attitude. It didn't seem like much could shake him. And he was really nice to the bartender and everybody around us. That's important too."

"Oh, no doubt. You can always tell a person by the way they treat people who take care of them."

As if on cue, our food arrives, and I dig into my pancakes, hoping by the time I finish them and the bacon sitting beside them, I'll feel less hungover and more alert to take on the task of getting ready for an important date.

I really don't want to mess this up—and not just for the sake of a book. I got a really good feeling about him. This isn't all trying to talk myself into liking him either. Trying to make him seem more special than he is so I can get into the act of writing yet another book.

The few minutes I spent with him last night were enough to show me the sort of man I want to be with. No, not wealthy—though that never hurts. He's kind and thoughtful, and he's good in a tight spot, which is an excellent quality for any man who dates me. I tend to get myself into tight spots.

"It's amazing," I manage around a mouthful of sweet, banana-studded pancake bliss.

"What is?" Hayley is a good girl today, eating an egg white omelet with steamed spinach and turkey sausage.

I swear, she just loves to show me up. Easy for her to eat that way—she didn't overdo it last night the way I did.

"The difference between fake confidence and the real deal. Paxton has real confidence. He's comfortable with himself. He doesn't have anything to prove. He's not one of those people who walks around, acting like he owns the world just because he has some money. He's not flashy about it. What's the word for that?"

"You're the writer."

I roll my eyes. "I can't think of the word right now, but he's not like that. He's just … chill. He's cool. A generally nice person."

"Boy, you're really swooning over him already, aren't you?" She shoots me a knowing look.

"No, not swooning. This isn't some Victorian melodrama. I'm not carrying smelling salts around."

"Maybe you need to."

"Wow, I'm so glad we're spending time together." I shove a piece of bacon into my mouth and chew obnoxiously. It gets on her nerves, which is obviously why I'm doing it.

"Could you not?"

"What? I'm only eating."

"You're such a baby sometimes. I mean, I love you, but we both know you're a hopeless romantic, and we also both know you wouldn't mind getting serious with somebody. Every time you start dating somebody new, there's always this hope that this could be the one that works out. Don't tell me I'm wrong."

"I won't because you aren't."

"I'm just saying, be careful. Take care of your heart. It's a pretty nice heart, and I like it. I don't want you getting all wrapped up in somebody so fast. Especially these really wealthy, business-minded people. You know they're on a whole other level.

"He's super handsome, super hot, and super wealthy, according to a quick skim of that article in *Forbes*. And from what you're telling me about him, he's also super awesome. Just the sort of guy who's easy to fall for."

I look down at my drink, stirring around what's left. "Why did I think a Bloody Mary and banana pancakes were a good combination?"

"Beats me."

Still staring, I admit, "Maybe I want to fall for somebody. This is, what, my seventh trope? That's seven guys I've dated in roughly a year. I'm bound to get a little black and blue. I'm bound to want to settle into something more with one of them. Why not Paxton?"

"Listen, I don't blame you. Just … maybe wait until after you go on an actual date together. It's one thing for us to drool over how good he looks in a pair of jeans and a cowboy hat—by the way, if there's ever an excuse to get him wearing nothing but those two things, you need to somehow manage to take a picture and send it to me, thanks in advance—and another for you to get all dreamy-eyed because he kept you from getting into a fistfight at a major fundraising event."

She's right. I know it.

"I will take your advice into consideration, Counselor."

And I do. All throughout the day, as I do my nails and curl my hair and try hard not to be too nervous, I remind myself to look at this in a big-picture sort of way. This is just one date. It doesn't have to mean anything more than that.

I mean, sure, he made me laugh. We're into the same sorts of movies.

And he has a pair of brown eyes I could sink into and never surface.

And, God, he's so tall! I never knew I had such a thing for tall men. Amazing, the things a girl can learn about herself when she's forced to date for the sake of her career.

It's with his height in mind that I slide into a pair of ambitious heels. They're a lot higher than anything I've worn recently—a solid four inches. Even that will put me half a foot shorter than him, but it will at least make things a little less awkward if he should, you know, decide to kiss me. Repeatedly.

Not that I have my hopes up or anything like that.

I have the ankle strap to the second shoe in place when there's a knock at the door. My heart just about jumps out of my chest, and instantly, I hate what I'm wearing.

Another knock. "Kitty?"

Oh, crap times two. It's Sunday night!

The only thing that keeps me from slapping my forehead as I hurry to the door—carefully tottering on these ridiculous heels—is knowing I'll leave a red mark on my head and Paxton will be here any minute.

When I open the door, Matt whistles as he takes in the full sight of me. "Wow. I didn't know our Sunday night takeout and TV watching got so fancy. I would've dressed up a little."

True, compared to my black dress and stilettos, his T-shirt and cargo shorts don't quite match up.

"I'm so sorry. I completely forgot."

He lifts an eyebrow. "You forgot? I mean, this is something we've been doing on Sunday nights for weeks."

"I know; I know. But things got crazy last night. I made a date for tonight with my new book subject, and I forgot it's Sunday and this is our thing."

"It got crazy at a charity ball? Man, I thought the bachelor auction was something. Maybe I need to go to more of these events."

"I really am sorry."

He shrugs, grinning. "It doesn't matter. It's just one night. If anything, I could catch up on some work."

I wag a finger at him. "Uh-oh. I think you're working too hard."

"I'll try not to make a habit of it." He follows me into the apartment, where I continue to get my stuff together. "So, who is this guy?"

"I met him last night at the ball." I have to laugh at myself. "Doesn't that sound weird? *I met him at a ball.*"

"So, he's the next guy you're writing about?"

"I hope so anyway." I look up from my purse and hold up crossed fingers.

"You know, maybe I'll go out tonight. Maybe I need to mix things up a bit. I've been spending too much time at home."

I look back at him while going through my purse to make sure I have what I need. *Where's my lip gloss?* "That's a good idea."

"You think so?"

"Sure! Why wouldn't I?" I look at him again and find him frowning. "What's wrong?"

"Hello?" There's a rap against the still-open door.

Matt and I both turn in time to see Paxton cautiously entering the apartment.

And, gosh, he looks so good that I forget to breathe all over again. Just like I did when I was looking at the pictures on Hayley's phone. Now, he's wearing a dark suit, the collar of his white shirt opened to reveal just a hint of tanned chest.

"Hi!" I squeak like a mouse. *Great, not the most confident way for that to come out.*

He smiles, completely dazzling me. "Hey there. Sorry I'm a little early."

"Don't worry about it. Punctuality is important, right?"

To my horror, Matt snickers. "Did you just figure that out?"

I shoot him a warning glare from behind Paxton as the two men approach each other. "This is my *friend*, Matt Ryder. He lives across the hall."

Did I emphasize the word *friend* a little too much? Maybe. But it's important to clarify things like that in times like this—when two men are eyeing each other as warily as these two are right now.

I swear, if he screws this up for me …

Paxton extends a hand. "Good to meet you. Paxton Cleary."

Something in Matt's face shifts. A muscle twitch, the slight flaring of his nostrils. "Cleary Oil, right?"

"You're familiar with us."

"Matt is a manager for a lot of high-profile clients and their investment portfolios," I explain.

Matt nods. "Sure, your name's been tossed around a lot lately."

Paxton pretends to wince and then chuckles. Almost. "So long as you aren't advising your clients to dump us."

Matt grins. "No. Not yet anyway."

"Okay!" *Time to get the hell out of here.* "I'm starving. What did you have in mind?" Meanwhile, I'm trying to usher Matt out of the apartment.

"I could go for a steak. Though you haven't eaten a truly good steak unless you've had one in Texas."

Matt chuckles as he crosses the hall to his door. "We know how to cook a steak up here in New

York too," he assures my date.

"We'll see." Paxton gives him a tight nod while I struggle with the lock on my door.

My palms are so sweaty that I can barely get the key into the lock without fumbling and almost dropping it.

What is it with these men when they meet Matt? Seriously, he's just my neighbor.

I don't breathe easily until we're on our way down the stairs and Matt is behind us.

What is it about him lately? Sure, it was thoughtless of me to forget to let him know about the change of plans tonight, but he's not usually like this.

"At least you don't have to worry about intruders and threats, living in the big city by yourself." Paxton casts a look up the stairs just before we turn on the landing to go down the next flight. "Not with a bulldog like that living across the hall."

I definitely need to change the subject. "What's it like outside? Should I have brought a wrap?"

"I think you'll be just fine with my arm wrapped around you," he states, tucking me under his arm as we walk out of the building.

Nothing like the perfect start to a first date—thanks to Matt—but Paxton's arm around me is already making it better.

Chapter Five

"SO, TELL ME more about yourself. I want to know all about you."

Darn it. Not that I'm against talking about myself per se, but it's so much more fun to listen to him. That slight twang to his voice is enough to melt me down to nothing. I would listen to him read the restaurant menu all night long if it came down to that.

Still, I can't refuse him, not when he's looking at me the way he is. The lighting in the restaurant is dim, the atmosphere sophisticated and quiet. There's definitely a sexy vibe around here too—one of those very masculine, very classy places with black walls and supple, high-backed leather booths. I feel like I have to speak in a whisper so as not to take away from the vibe.

"I'm a pretty simple person." I shrug. "As we established last night, I don't fit in very well with my grandmother's crowd."

"You did establish that, yes." His mouth twitches, like he's trying to hold back a smile.

"I'm a writer, which you probably overheard

last night as well."

"I did overhear that. I understand you write"—he finally smiles—"romance. Not filth."

"It's amazing how just you saying that word puts me right back in that moment."

"I'm sorry." He gets serious again. "Honestly, I'm not trying to antagonize you. The whole thing sounds pretty silly to me. You were right to call her out for being a hypocrite. I know a lot of women like her, and you hit the nail on the head. The ones with the biggest trust funds are the first ones to tell other people how to live their lives. The hypocrisy can be downright staggering."

I can't help myself. "You know a lot of women like her?"

He's cool rather than rising to the bait. "I've known my share. Which is why I'm out with you right now and not one of them."

I still can't help myself. "I saw a few trying to catch your eye last night. That blonde even pretended to stumble, so she could fall into you at the bar."

His head snaps back slightly. "Is that what that was about? I thought she'd tripped."

"Please. I'm surprised you have any feeling in your arm after the way she was holding on to you last night."

"You're observant." He's chuckling as he raises his glass of scotch. "I suppose that comes with the territory of being a writer though. You get to observe people and put them into your books."

This is it. This is when I have to tell the truth. Isn't it? I mean, that's the only fair thing to do.

He deserves to know he might end up in a book if this goes anywhere, which I most sincerely hope it will because just sitting across the table from him has my nerves sizzling, my heart fluttering. It's like being a teenager with a crush. I have to remind myself that eye contact is not a bad thing, that I should stop blushing and looking away when he tries to hold me in place with that penetrating stare of his.

"It's funny you should mention that. I'm in the process of getting started with my new book right now. And it might hit close to home for you—the main character, I mean."

"How so?"

Might as well get the whole thing out of the way now. I take another sip of my drink before launching into a shortened version of the story, but this time, I decide to not go so far back.

I simply say, "My editor wanted to change my image a bit and asked me to write about leading men from different walks of life."

He leans back against the booth, nodding slowly. "And this time, you have to write about, what?"

I cringe a little. "A cowboy."

"I see. So, the reason you were interested in me last night was for the sake of a book?"

"Oh God, no!" I rush out.

"I was only kidding," he whispers. "I'm the one who approached you, remember?"

Oh. Right. "That wasn't funny."

"You're right. It wasn't. Can you forgive me?"

"I guess so." I give him a little shrug. "I do have to write a book after all."

He has a very nice laugh, the kind of laugh that gives a person no other choice but to join in. "Hey, what man wouldn't want to be the subject of a romance novel?"

"It wouldn't be you exactly. But I need to re-search, you know? Learn about your business, find out the sort of things you do. People want to dismiss romance, but it involves just as much research and care as any other genre."

"I have no doubt. And I respect your hard work." He leans in closer, eyes sparkling in the candlelight. "Are you sure there aren't any other ways I could provide inspiration?"

Yep, there's that tingle again. Only now, I have the real thing in front of me, not just a picture. I manage to catch my breath enough to whisper, "Well, that depends on how you feel about after-hours research. I would never want to assume."

My entire body lights up like he just touched a match to a flame. I can't believe this is happening. I'm sitting here, blatantly flirting with this guy, and he doesn't mind knowing there's a book at stake.

"I'm afraid my after-hours services as a consult-ant on this work of fiction will require compensation." He folds his hands on top of the table, sitting up straighter, like we're suddenly negotiating in a boardroom.

"And just what should this compensation consist of?"

"I think you'll find it pretty standard. Frequent meals together while I'm in town this week. The occasional hand-holding. Maybe a peck on the cheek when I drop you off at home."

It's a real struggle, keeping a straight face. "I think that can be arranged. Your terms are more than fair."

"I think so."

I tip my head to the side. "Of course, I was prepared to give you a lot more than that. If only you had asked for it."

He leans in, winking conspiratorially. "Haven't you ever heard of renegotiating contracts further down the line?"

"I'm sorry, but my terms are final."

The tips of his fingers skim the back of my hand. "There's always room for renegotiation, darlin'."

Darlin'. He called me *darlin'*, just like out of a cowboy movie.

"Have you decided?" Our server waits nearby with an expectant smile.

I guess she wouldn't appreciate if I asked for a bed. Or even a couch in the back room. Hell, I would settle for a secluded booth because I want this man. Just the way he's touching the back of my hand has me yearning for more.

Somehow, I manage to get through dinner without bursting into flames or melting into a puddle, and we are now in the car, headed back to my apartment.

"I know this sounds like the oldest excuse in the book, but I truly do have an early meeting in the morning."

I only shake my head with a smirk. "Please. Don't try to pull the oldest line in the book on a writer."

"How can I make it up to you?" He helps me out of his car, and we leave the driver waiting out front while we dash up the steps and then up to my floor.

"You have nothing to make up to me. After a dinner like that?" I might not eat again for a week, but it was worth it. And much like when I dated Blake Marlin, my billionaire boss, there weren't any prices on the menu. At least this time, I knew what to expect.

"But you did want to learn more about me, right?"

"Of course, but we have all week." I narrow my eyes to slits when we reach my front door. "Unless you were planning on ghosting me after tonight."

"Damn it." He snaps his fingers with a frown. "You figured out my whole plan."

"Laugh all you want, but it wouldn't be the first time a guy did that to a girl."

"Not this guy, little lady." Before I know it, he has my face between his hands, and he isn't laughing anymore. "No, Kitty, I have no intention of ghosting you after tonight. Book or no book."

"I'm glad," I whisper. "Book or no book."

His eyes. Oh God, his eyes. I start to drown in them, but his hands on my face and his thumbs stroking my cheekbones pull me closer, and I'm saved as his mouth catches mine in the sweetest, most tender kiss that still somehow sparks a blaze in my core. All of him is in this kiss. It's slow, skillful, the kiss of a man who knows who he is and what he wants and how to make a girl feel wanted and safe and taken care of.

His slow kiss turns into a heated frenzy of emotions, and it takes all the self-control I possess not to wrap my legs around him and take him to the floor. Just as I'm in need of air, he pulls back.

"Wow." He clears his throat after what feels like an hour of kissing. "I sincerely wish I didn't have to be up before the sun."

"Me too." I can barely stay on my feet; I'm so dizzy and winded. There can't possibly be enough blood in my brain, what with all of it having traveled further south.

"I guess it's for the best that I leave you now." He glances across the hall. "I wouldn't want your bulldog getting upset."

"He's a good guy. Protective but good."

"Hmm." He looks at me, brows raised. "All

righty then. I'd better be going before the driver gets a ticket for sitting out there. What are you doing tomorrow night?"

I'd jump up and down if it wasn't for these shoes. Knowing me, I'd break an ankle. "Getting together with you, if possible."

"That's what I wanted to hear. What would you like to do? I don't get to the city much, only one or two times before now, so all I know about it is what I've seen on TV and in the movies."

"Leave it to me then." I stand on my very tippy-toes to give him a kiss on the cheek and take a deep whiff of his cologne. It's so masculine and musky and sexy; it drives me crazy.

It's only when I'm alone in my apartment and the blood has flowed back to my brain that it hits me.

I have no idea what to do with a cowboy in the city.

Chapter Six

"WOW. YOU REALLY knocked it out of the park this time."

"Thank you?" It feels kind of strange, accepting congratulations for the fact that Paxton happens to be gorgeous. I didn't have anything to do with that.

"I'm just saying, if you don't end up walking bowlegged after riding him or a horse—or preferably both at different times—when this is all over, there's no hope for you."

"Maggie"—I laugh—"you're too much." I've come to expect it from my editor.

"Is he going to take you home to see how he lives?"

"One thing at a time," I beg. "I'm just glad last night went well. He's a very sweet guy."

"And sexy as hell."

"Yes, that helps too."

"Let's see …" I can just about hear her tapping her nails on her desk as she ponders. "I think it would be fabulous to have sex in a barn, in the hay."

"Fabulous? I mean, aren't barns kind of smelly

sometimes?"

"Come on. You can't tell me the notion of being completely swept up in the moment—even if the moment takes place in a smelly barn—doesn't appeal to you. Having this Paxton throw you down on the hay and tear your clothes off because he can't be bothered to keep his hands off you for another minute."

Okay, she might have a point.

"Maybe you'll get really lucky and visit him when there are a bunch of men running around, working the farm, all sweaty and dirty, using their muscles and … sweating."

"You already mentioned the sweating part."

"It's important."

I can't believe I'm about to ask her this, but she started it. "You aren't one of those people who are into, you know, body stuff? Are you? Like, really sweaty, stinky men? No judgment."

She bursts out laughing. "No! But all those muscular guys glistening in the sun? Come on, Valentine. Use your writer's imagination."

"Fair enough." And to be honest, I certainly wouldn't mind seeing Paxton out there, doing all those sweaty, glistening things she's talking about.

"Have you ever considered doing it on a tractor?"

"Okay, let's get something straight. He lives on a ranch, for one thing, not a farm. I don't even know if they use tractors. But even if they do, just because you want me to write a certain kind of scene in the book doesn't mean that scene has to play out in real life. There are a lot of things I'm willing to do, but I don't know about doing it out in the open. Sorry to disappoint you." Not for the first time do I wonder why the woman has such an interest in my sex life.

"Okay, okay."

"You're the one who just gave me the line about my writer's imagination."

"I said, okay." She clicks her tongue. "You need to live a little."

"I'll keep that in mind." I certainly will not.

Circumstances would have to be absolutely perfect for me to even consider something like that. We'd have to be miles away from anybody else. I wouldn't even want there to be any animals nearby. Nobody wants to be stared at by, like, a cow or horse or something while they're doing it.

Amazing, the way the mind works. Because the second I have that thought, the image of Phoebe floats through my mind. Sitting on the floor by the bed, watching me with her big golden retriever eyes and wondering why I make such funny faces while in the throes of passion.

Only there wouldn't be any reason for that to happen since her owner and I would never engage in anything like that. No way, not a chance, never going to happen. Matt and I once shared a bed and, yes, I was naked and, yes, that was entirely my fault. But it'll never happen again.

So, why did I think about her just then? Probably because she's the only animal anywhere nearby.

"Well, you know I'll be waiting with bated breath. Enjoy yourself. Just don't enjoy yourself so much that you forget you're writing a book," she adds.

I guess the *it's all my fault you're burned out* Maggie is gone.

"Yes, ma'am," I say before ending the call.

Now, there's only one problem: how to keep the perfect man interested in me long enough to get anything worth writing about out of the deal.

"Because that's what you're in this for," I remind myself while going to the kitchen for something to drink. "You're writing a book. You're not trying to form a deep, lasting connection. You are dating. You are having fun. Don't put unnecessary pressure on the poor guy."

It doesn't help my current problem though. What was I thinking, offering to take the reins tonight? I don't have the first idea what he'll be interested in. Sure, he's a nice guy, and he seems pretty down-to-earth. Everybody has their limits, don't they?

Pacing around the apartment doesn't help. It's early afternoon, so Hayley will be neck deep in work. Not like it matters what time of day it is. She's always busy, chronically busy. I'm sure if I were to ask her what I should do, she would tell me to put on my skimpiest lingerie and greet him at the front door, wearing that and a smile.

Good idea, but maybe not the direction I want to go tonight.

Who else can I ask? Matt might be finished with the bulk of his work for the day since he gets started so early in the morning, but I can't see going to him with this problem. He's probably still mad at me for missing our takeout-and-binge ritual.

And honestly, the more I remember what happened last night when Paxton first got here, I'm not sure I want to talk to Matt right now either. He can't run around, acting like a moody child, and not expect at least a little pushback. Completely unnecessary, the way he acted. Like he had a personal grudge against Paxton.

So, he's out too.

Hayley's right. I need to expand my circle of friends.

The notion occurs to me that I might go to my social media accounts and ask my readers what they would do. That's actually not a bad idea even if I don't end up taking any of the advice they give me. One of the things I struggled with most during my two-week hiatus was how to keep my readers engaged. Frankly, I've never cared too much for social media. Not past high school anyway. We all lived on our phones at one point in our lives.

Things were different back then too. More fun, more social. It seems like all I find online anymore is stress and fighting. Not so much fun to be had there.

I post the question anyway, asking my followers to chime in with their ideas for the perfect date for a cowboy. This is most definitely a hint at the subject of my next book, which isn't a bad thing either. It's never too soon to start drumming up interest in the next project.

Keeping in mind that I will not likely find anything usable in the responses I receive, I turn to the only other person I would consider asking real advice from.

"She isn't home, I'm afraid." Peter chuckles softly. "Monday afternoons are when she has lunch with her friends."

"Of course. I forgot. It's easy to get the days mixed up when you pretty much do the same thing every day."

"She tells me you met someone at the ball. See, I was right to suggest you go in my place."

"Yes, that was very generous of you." He can't see me rolling my eyes, so I don't bother holding back for his sake. "That's the reason I was calling. I'm a little nervous about seeing him again tonight."

"Why? Is he a decent type of man?"

"Oh, sure, he's great. I just … I offered to come up with something to do tonight, and I'm completely at a loss. I don't know what to do that he wouldn't find, you know … pedestrian. Boring."

"Oh, I see. That is a tricky one." He pauses. "Does he strike you as being a snob?"

"Not at all actually. He's the complete opposite. I don't think I've ever known anybody so real and easygoing."

Blake was a really nice, cool guy, but even he had his pretentiousness. Granted, I don't know Paxton very well yet, but I very much get the feeling he's more at home in a pair of jeans than in a tuxedo.

"Did the two of you do any talking about your personal interests? Was it all about business?"

"No, we talked about the things we like. Granted, I'm not really a college football fan, and I've never been hunting. But he likes movies. Old ones in particular."

"Is he very familiar with the city?"

"No, in fact, he said he's only been up here one or two times for business. It's just recently that his father has had him traveling around to their different offices."

"Well, for what it's worth, I know what I would like to do if I were the lucky young man going out with you tonight."

"You sweet-talker. Save that for my grandmother."

His laughter echoes in the large, spacious room. I'm not sure which one he's in, but they're all pretty big. "Come on. Do you think she falls for that sort of talk?"

"Good point." I giggle. "Of course, I want to hear what you would want to do. Your opinion means a lot to me."

"I'm honored to hear that. So, if I love old films and I've only been to New York one or two times, it might be fun to take a short tour of different locations that were made famous by a movie they were in."

"Oh, that's a great idea!"

"You aren't just saying that to make me feel better?"

"Not at all! No, it's a genius idea. I can make it into a goofy kind of touristy night. We could do silly things, go sightseeing. That's perfect!"

"I'm glad I could help." There's so much warmth in his voice; I can tell he's pleased.

What's even better is the handful of readers who commented on my post, suggesting the exact same thing—at least, close enough. Acting like tourists, being tacky and terrible, showing him how we do it in the big city. More than one also suggests having a cowboy ride a horse through Times Square, but I can't imagine that wouldn't come with its own logistical challenges.

A touristy night it is.

Though really, I need to see the man on horseback in person at least once before I draw my final breath. I don't ask much from life. Just little things like this.

Chapter Seven

"Sorry we couldn't get the actual table from the movie."

Frankly, it's amazing we got a table at all, but that's usually the case at Katz's. The place is famous for more than an actress faking an orgasm at one of its tables.

Paxton shrugs this off while taking off his suede jacket. It's gotten a little cool, more typical for April than the warmth of the past week. "You sure they're going to have enough food here for a guy with a big appetite like mine?"

The man has a point. Last night, I watched him devour a bowl of French onion soup, a porterhouse steak, loaded baked potato, probably two-thirds of an order of lobster mac and cheese—which we shared—and not to mention the wedge salad with bacon and bleu cheese, which he ate before our entrées arrived.

Even so, the fact that he feels he has to ask a question like that tells me the man has no idea what he's in for.

"Trust me." I nod to a man on his way past our

table, carrying a pastrami sandwich roughly as big as my head.

"Oh. Okay. Now, we're talking."

"Have you ever had pastrami?"

"No, ma'am."

"Trust me, you'll be in heaven."

"I leave myself entirely in your hands."

"Careful what you say. I might take you seriously."

"Who says I don't want you to take me seriously?"

The man needs to watch himself, talking like that. My poor heart can only take so much, and it's already racing, just being near him. That's all it takes, just being in his presence.

I take the liberty of ordering for both of us before joining him at the table again since it's much easier for me to go up to the counter than it would be for him. The tables are pushed together so tight that even somebody a lot smaller than the broad, rangy rancher—like myself—has to turn sideways and inch along between tables loaded with corned beef, matzo ball soup, and countless other mouth-watering temptations.

It's a relief to get back to our table. "I hope you aren't claustrophobic. Guess I should have asked that in advance."

"Good thing I'm not afraid of heights either." His smile is almost goofy, boyish. "You hear about the top of the Empire State Building all the time, right? I figure it can't possibly be as cool, being up there, as what you hear. I mean, how many things live up to their reputation?"

"That's very insightful."

"I've seen a lot of things, and I've been let down a lot of times."

"I hope you aren't bored or disappointed with tonight."

He frowns. "Why would I be? Isn't it obvious that I'm having a great time with you?"

I can feel the flush of my cheeks, and I absolutely hate it. "I was pretty worried about tonight. I was afraid I'd bitten off more than I could chew, inviting you out with no idea what a man like you would find entertaining."

"A man like me?" He rubs a hand along the side of his face, catching a little bit of stubble that is so sexy that I can hardly stand it. "And just who is a man like me?"

"Don't." I laugh. "Don't put me on the spot."

"I'm not trying to. I'm just wondering what you're thinking." He grins. "Remember, you're the one writing the book. If you're going into this with preconceived notions about a so-called man like me, we should seriously talk about it. All joking aside. You assume that because my daddy owns an oil company he inherited from his daddy, I won't be interested in doing things like this?"

"Have you ever been to a Jewish deli before?"

"That's not a fair question since I've never seen

one near where I live."

"Fine, but don't tell me you don't travel. There's nothing wrong with being more familiar with the sort of restaurants we went to last night than with a deli even if it's famous."

"That doesn't mean I'm not interested in other experiences. Nothing could be further from the truth. Sometimes, we just need somebody in our life to open our eyes to these adventures. This is exactly the sort of thing I would've liked to do if I had thought of it myself. You're a genius."

"In all honesty, I asked for advice."

"Then, who should I thank for this? Because it's already some of the most fun I've had in a long time."

"Peter." Paxton furrows his brows and I continue. "Remember how we met?"

"How could I forget?" he asks with a grin.

"We didn't talk much about Peter. He's the one I almost got into a fight over, and he's worth it. He worked for my grandmother for over thirty years as her go-to guy. Butler, chauffeur, you name it. He took care of her. Eventually, he fell in love with her. And as it turns out, she fell in love with him too."

"That's a beautiful story."

"I think so. But not everybody shares that opinion. I've never seen my grandmother so happy and content. If anything, it seems like the natural next step to me—they were practically a couple in every other way, you know? He was already looking after her, making sure she had everything she needed. Sometimes, I think he knows her better than she knows herself."

"That's very sweet." His expression changes, turning into more of a frown. "Though why would any of those catty types care about two people being a great match if one of them started out as a domestic servant?"

"The rich don't enter relations with the help. Haven't you heard of that rule?"

He leans in like this interests him. "See, that's what you gotta remember about me. I'm not one of these highfalutin types. My daddy made sure none of his kids ended up walking around, acting like we had silver spoons in our mouths. We all had to work hard on the ranch and in the oil fields. I got to know the men I was working alongside. One in particular who worked the ranch taught me how to train horses for the rodeo. That's more my passion than being stuck in an office. It's something I took interest in and enjoy doing in my free time. As you can guess, I appreciate the value of hard work. You don't have to worry about hanging out with me. I'm just as much at home, cracking open a beer and watching a game."

"I hope you mean that." I catch the eye of the deli worker signaling me from behind the counter— and behind a veritable mountain of food. "Because I'm about to test that theory."

Moments later, here we are. Sitting with what's

probably close to two pounds of juicy meat between us along with two bowls of matzo ball soup, latkes, and blintzes—my personal favorite.

It's almost too much for the table to hold.

"Wow!" Paxton's eyes bulge once everything's set down between us.

"So, is the big Texas cowboy impressed with the selection?"

He takes a bite of his pastrami and closes his eyes. "Oh, dear Lord. Where has this been all my life?"

"Right here in New York." My corned beef is a revelation, too, but that's no surprise.

He ends up eating the second half, which I can't possibly touch, thanks to eating what I could of the first half. We both finish our soup, and he expresses appreciation for the latkes before digging into the cheese blintzes with me.

"I need to come here more often, though I'm afraid all my suits would have to be let out." He pats his extremely firm tummy with a satisfied smile once we've both gorged ourselves beyond all measure.

"Don't worry. We have a ton of walking ahead of us."

"I'd have to walk all the way home to burn that off, I'm afraid." He shoots me a wicked grin before we get up from the table. "So, you don't plan on reenacting that scene from the movie? Throwing your head back and faking ecstasy?"

I snort, like this doesn't make me go tingly all over. Just the fact that he's talking about it. "I never fake ecstasy."

His brows lift. "Hmm. I'll keep that in mind."

I don't know how much more of this flirtation I can handle before taking him into the nearest alleyway and having my way with him. And to think, I thought it was a repulsive notion with Dustin.

The cool night air helps calm the flush on my cheeks as we step outside to catch a cab to Times Square.

"Oh, this is impressive." Paxton looks genuinely excited, too, when we pull to a stop in front of the Cohan Statue and hop out of the car.

"It's the center of the whole world, so they say." I never would've imagined having so much fun, simply watching Paxton—this huge, handsome, sophisticated man who grew up as an heir to an oil empire—looking downright gobsmacked by everything.

"This is where the ball drops on New Year's. I've watched it so many times." He flashes one of those goofy smiles of his, and I'm hooked.

I can't help it. Never have I met a man I've wanted to climb like a tree while also wanting to cuddle and protect his sweet, innocent heart.

"I can't believe you've never visited before. Your family's had offices here for a long time, haven't they?"

His smile slips a little. "You've been doing your research."

"Hey, I'm a New York girl. I don't randomly date anybody if I can help it. That's what Google is for."

"Fair enough. No, I haven't been here for business until this trip. Daddy kept me down on the ranch and in the fields, like I said earlier. It's only been the last year or so that I've been moving into the business end of things. I can understand the method behind his madness. He wanted to make sure I had a firm grasp on the work before turning toward the business."

"That's smart. How many businesses have been run into the ground by heirs who didn't understand the first thing about it?"

"Exactly." He winds an arm around mine, and I don't stop him. "You're a fascinating person. Anybody ever told you that?"

"Not recently. I think my grandmother finds me fascinating but not in the way you'd think."

"Come on. She smiled at you with all the pride of a grandma who's happy to have a granddaughter like you. Who wouldn't be proud?" When I wave a dismissive hand, he shakes his head. "You're a *New York Times* best-selling author!"

"Oh? Look who's been doing his research."

He laughs it off. "Yeah, well, you're not the only one who can't go around, dating just anybody."

"I'm glad to know I passed muster."

"You did better than that." We come to a stop in pretty much the center of everything. It's as bright as day out here with so many billboards, signs, news tickers. "So, what did you have in mind here?"

"Well, since you're a newbie to the city, I thought we'd give you the true tourist experience." With that, I pull him into a shop full of souvenirs. T-shirts, hats, giant sunglasses with NYC written across the lenses—not sure how much good that does, basically blinding whoever's wearing them.

"This is … charmin'." Paxton finds a foam hat in the shape of the Statue of Liberty's crown and plops it on his head with a serious expression.

I have to take a second to compose myself.

"Here. The look's not complete yet." I find a few strings of plastic beads with plastic American flags threaded in-between and have him bend down, so I can put them around his neck. There's a giant pair of sunglasses with apple-shaped frames, so I slide them on him and then drape a scarf with the word *fuhgeddaboudit* written all over it.

"What's that mean?" He laughs after trying to pronounce it.

"Come on." I hold my hand up, fingers joined together and pointed upward. "Fuhgeddaboudit, ya know?" I sneer in my best impression of a Hollywood-style mafioso.

It's his turn to laugh at me until he almost falls over.

"Okay, I didn't think it was that funny."

"You're adorable."

"I'm glad you think so since I'm buying all of this junk for you and I fully expect you to wear it outside."

He shrugs. "Sounds good to me."

"You're serious?" I can barely contain myself.

"Sure. If you're buying, I'll wear this very classy ensemble outside. Why not?"

I waste no time in getting to the register, where the unamused clerk rings up each price tag with the same blank expression. I guess they get a lot of people like us here. We only think we're being silly and outrageous.

When we get outside, the effect is incredible. Here's this six-foot-five hunk of man with shoulders wide enough that I wonder how he makes it through a doorway without turning sideways, wearing this ridiculous getup. He's impossible to miss.

"I can't believe you're actually wearing that." I can't stop giggling every time I look up at him.

The foam crown really brings the look together—and makes him that much more visible.

"I feel more myself than I have this entire trip," he assures me. "Really. This is a freeing experience. I might wear this sort of thing all the time. Who's to say?"

"Now, I think there's something in that foam that's leaking into your brain."

"I wish I could blame it on the foam, but no. This is me." He holds his arms out, stopping in his tracks under a billboard for the latest Broadway hit.

"Hey! Can we get a picture?" A pair of girls runs over to us, positioning themselves, one under each outstretched arm. One of them hands me her phone. "Please?"

I look at Paxton, ready for him to brush them off. I mean, fun is fun, but this is ridiculous. He's not some Times Square attraction, the way some people are in their off-brand cartoon costumes.

"Sure!" He wraps an arm around their shoulders and smiles from ear to ear.

I can't believe what I'm doing as I take the picture and hand the phone back.

"Who are you?" I ask when it's just the two of us again. "I expected … I don't know what I expected exactly, but it wasn't you. I never would've imagined an oil baron's son posing with strangers in the middle of the square, wearing way overpriced tourist junk."

"This is the most fun I've had in years, I swear." He stops again, taking me by the hand and pulling me in. "There's this picture from Times Square that's pretty famous …"

I don't have time to catch up to what he's getting at before he has me bent back over his arm. I barely even have time to close my eyes before he's kissing me just like in the old photo of the sailor and the nurse.

Chapter Eight

By the time we reach Central Park, Paxton is carrying his getup. It's one thing to wear it in the square with so many bright lights and passing cars and people taking goofy pictures.

Not that the park is any less crowded on a night like this. The perfect night for a walk, clear and cool.

"I guess you don't need to be told there's been, like, a million movie scenes shot here."

"I've gotta admit, I had no idea it was so big."

"Oh, sure. You could walk around every day for a week and find something new every time."

"Isn't it dangerous at night?"

"It used to be a lot worse back in the day—at least, that's the way my parents made it sound whenever I asked if I could hang out here with my friends. Back before I was born, it must've been much worse."

"My mama was very cautious with her boys. Wanted us to be strong and tough but didn't so much want us to get out there with the oil workers, risking getting hurt."

"I'm sure that couldn't have been easy for any of

you to deal with."

He grins. "Daddy wouldn't have it. She was acting like a woman—like a fool, I guess he meant. I don't share that opinion," he's quick to add.

"I hope not."

"Nah, Daddy's in the past. It's what I've been trying to tell him for a long time. He didn't settle down until he was in his late forties. I was born just after his fifty-first birthday, and I'm the oldest."

"He's that old?" I have to clap a hand over my mouth after that one.

His eyes widen. "Uh, yeah, he is."

"Sorry," I whisper, cringing. "I saw him at the ball, and I thought he was in his sixties."

"He's the healthiest person in the world—if you listen to him anyway." He snickers. There's fondness there though; it's obvious. "He takes an ice-cold shower every morning of his life, gets plenty of fresh air and exercise. He also smokes cigars, laughs at the idea of eating vegetables, and drinks a glass of whiskey after dinner every night. If not more."

"You must have good genes in your family."

"That's the truth. His daddy was a hundred and three when he passed, and the one before that was in his late nineties and on his fourth wife by the time he went toes up."

"Strong stock? Is that what they call it?"

"Yeah, that's what they call it. You sound like a rancher already."

"I'm a quick study."

Somehow, his hand finds mine, and that's nice. Strolling together like this with the glow of countless lamps lighting our way, we might as well be in an old Hollywood romance.

Except for the kids goofing off on their skateboards and a random dog pooping not far from where we're walking. Things like that never happened in the old movies.

"What does the rest of your week look like?" he asks in a soft voice.

"I'll be working whenever I can get the words down. Otherwise, I don't do much."

He lets out a snort like he doesn't believe me. "No way."

"Yes way." I shoot him a look. "Why so skeptical?"

"You're in the middle of the whole world here. There has to be a thousand things to do every night."

"I'm sure there is," I allow. "I'm more of a homebody. I probably work too much, and most of that work ends up getting done at night. The actual writing part anyway. I edit myself better during the day."

"I admire your dedication. Not everybody can push themselves to work so hard without a boss breathing down their neck. I wish I had a handful of people like you working under me."

"I do have an editor who does her fair share of

breathing down my neck now that you mention it, but I know it could be much worse. She's not a micromanager, thank goodness. I can't stand being micromanaged."

"Another way we're alike. It drives my father crazy when I push back on the way he wants to manage everything. It's time for him to step down, you know?" He lets me lead him down another path, taking us closer to the pond.

"I bet he doesn't like that much."

The man I observed at the ball was boisterous, magnetic, energetic.

"If you want to put it mildly, no. He doesn't like it. But he's back in the past. His thinking, his methods. We're suffering because he won't …"

I wait for more, but he goes silent for a long time. After the way he raised his voice, the sudden silence is deafening.

"I'm sorry," he eventually sighs. "I didn't mean to get worked up. I tend to do that when I'm talking about him, about the business."

"You don't have to apologize. And if there's anything you want to get off your chest, I promise it won't end up in any book ever." I make an X over my chest with one finger.

He holds my hand a little tighter. "Thanks. But really, I'm not out with you to talk about work. Any man stupid enough to waste time with you on complaining about work is too stupid to run a company, I'll tell you that much."

"You should be the writer. You have a way with words."

I look across the water, toward Gapstow Bridge. "You should see it out here in winter. When there's snow on the ground, in the trees. When everything is so still and quiet from the snow muffling the noise. Sometimes, you can actually hear the flakes landing. It's incredible."

"It sounds incredible."

We sit on a bench, facing the water. It seems natural, leaning against him. Letting his arm close around my shoulders. Letting my head touch that shoulder, resting it there.

It's probably wrong to let myself fall for him so soon. I know it.

But I can't help it. He's as close to perfect as I've ever known in my entire life. He makes me laugh, makes me feel good, just by being with me. He can laugh at himself. He's smart, and he knows who he is.

And oh my goodness, he makes my body hum, when he looks at me.

Like now, when I look up into his eyes.

"You know, you're the most beautiful girl I've ever met," he murmurs while taking my chin in his hand.

"I doubt it."

"It's not a line." He tips his head to the side. "You think I would pull an ordinary line on a writer? I'm smarter than that."

It gets a smile out of me anyway. "Thank you then."

"That's better. You'd need to learn to accept a compliment if you're planning to spend any time with me. I believe in appreciating the good things in my life."

"Am I a good thing in your life?" I wish it were easier to breathe. I wish it were harder to fall into the dark brown pools of light that are his eyes. I can't help myself. I can't even look away.

"So far, so good." He lowers his head an inch and then another. "And getting better all the time."

It's like it was before but even hotter. Not so tentative this time.

And we're sitting, which helps. I don't have to worry about him kissing me until I'm so breathless that I swoon in his arms.

Though he is leaving me breathless, kissing me slowly, passionately. I run my hand over his scruffy cheek before letting my fingers slide into his thick, soft hair. His breath catches a little, which only makes my breath catch.

There's nothing in the world but him. But us. I can't get enough of his taste, his smell. The feeling of his lips moving against mine, the strong arm wrapped around me, pulling me closer until there's no space between us at all.

And that's still not enough. I'm hungry for him, starving for a real man in my life. Now that I have him with me here and now, I'm not about to let it go to waste.

"Do you have an early meeting?" I whisper as he kisses my cheek, my throat.

"Not this time." It's a growl, deep and full of promise.

My heart somehow manages to beat even faster, which shouldn't be possible since it's already pounding out of my chest.

"Good." I catch his mouth again and bury both hands in his hair this time.

The way he groans is like magic, heating me from the inside out, like no actual fire could ever do.

Then, his phone rings, and he groans louder. And a little less sexily. "Damn it. Hang on."

I wait while he fishes the phone from his jacket.

"Energetic or not, when your father's in his eighties, you answer every call."

"Understood." I would feel the same way about my grandmother, especially after the scare with her heart attack.

He stands and takes a few steps away. His answers to whoever's on the other end are short. I can't get a read on what's happening. Whatever it is can't be all that great.

"Fine." He slides the phone into his pocket. I watch as his shoulders rise and fall.

I finally have to ask, "Is everything okay?"

"Just great." He turns to me with a shrug. "My father. He wants to go over numbers for a meeting we're going into tomorrow morning. Says it can't wait until breakfast."

My heart sinks. There goes any chance of having fun tonight. "Oh. I see."

"And I feel like the world's biggest ass."

"Don't. Don't!" I get up and go to him, sliding my arms around his waist. "You were in town for business before we met, right? You can't forget all about your responsibilities because of me. Even if I want you to."

"You're killing me," he groans before kissing the top of my head. "Next time. And I'm saying that because I'll die if I don't get to spend some alone time with you soon."

"We'll have to keep that in mind." I step back, taking his hand. "Come on. Responsibilities call."

Though I sincerely wish we both weren't so darn responsible.

Chapter Nine

HE TOUCHED HER cheek. Her skin sizzled from the slight contact.

"What is it about you?" he asked in the softest whisper.

"What do you mean?"

"I mean, you make me want to forget about everything in the world but you."

She laughed. "I'm talented like that."

Her laughter only covered up what she wanted to say. There weren't any words for it—at least none she knew—so it would've been an embarrassing waste of time, trying to explain how he made her feel.

What he made her feel. Like it was possible to find somebody who saw and understood her.

Not to mention what he did to her in other ways. Physical ways. He didn't even need to touch her to make her insides flutter, to start a fire deep in her core. A small fire but a healthy one. It smoldered until bursting into full life at the touch of his hand.

"I want to take you home to the ranch. I want to show you my life. My family. And I would love to see you on horseback."

She gulped. Horseback? He expected her to do that

when she hadn't so much as ridden a bike in years—and even then, it had been a lot of years. Like, since she had worn braces.

"That sounds amazing," she whispered instead. "I would love that."

Because aside from the notion of riding a massive horse, it did sound like something she would love to do. Knowing he wanted her to meet his family, to know his life, was sweeter than anything she could imagine.

Until he kissed her.

"No, no." I mutter a few choice curses before deleting the whole passage. It's terrible, awful, and it doesn't come close to scratching the surface of what I felt last night.

Or rather, what my heroine should feel while gazing into the eyes of the man she's already starting to fall in love with.

I wish there were a way to describe how I felt, being with him. How special he made everything feel. Even something like walking through the park was better, elevated, thanks to him. Everything seemed sort of sparkly. Shimmery.

Yes, I am most definitely in the grip of some serious crushing.

I'm also a writer, for heaven's sake. I should be able to describe the feeling of walking around with a truly incredible person whose pants I want to tear off.

Certain things aren't so easy to describe. Especially when a person is in the middle of them, all tangled up in emotion and hormones.

I've been working on this scene all day, and nothing's coming together. It doesn't flow; it sounds stilted when I read it aloud. This sort of setback happens all the time. It's certainly not Paxton's fault.

It's mine. Because I'm the worst writer who ever put a word on paper. What right do I have to even call myself a published author? Sure, I've been published. Okay. But still. Maybe I need to hang up my laptop and call it a day.

The knock on the door couldn't have come at a better time.

"Please, whoever you are, come in and kill me."

The door opens slowly.

"Uh, you okay?"

I barely lift my head from my folded arms to find Matt standing halfway inside the apartment. "Do I look okay? Do I sound okay?"

"You've been talking to yourself all day. I've heard the word *hack* thrown around to the point where I was afraid it wasn't about work anymore and you were about to hack somebody to pieces."

"Those were the times when I was throwing myself on the bed, trying not to actually scream. I wish somebody would hack me to pieces." I slump even further down in my chair until I'm practically under the desk.

"I thought so, and I figured you might want a happy distraction."

Before I have the chance to ask if he considers himself a happy distraction, he opens the door wider, and in bounds Phoebe.

Darn it, he knows me. My spirits pick up instantly. How can I help it when I'm getting doggy kisses?

"Hey, beautiful girl!"

"She was worried about you over here, calling yourself a hack and cursing all day."

"She's a very insightful dog." I scratch her behind the ears, which she loves. "I don't know where I'd be without her."

"I guess things aren't going well."

"Good guess." I scowl at the laptop before turning to Phoebe again. She's got her paws up on my knee, sniffing for snacks on the desk. "Sorry, girl, I already finished the popcorn."

"Don't let her fool you. She just had her dinner." He takes a seat on the sofa, not far from me, and settles in without being asked whether it's okay. And that's the friendship level we've reached.

But this is the first time I've seen or spoken to him since Sunday night.

"I should have her do the writing for me. It might turn out better."

"This is how it always goes, and you know it."

"Not true."

"True enough. Every time you've written a new book in the last year, you've hit this point, where you think it's never good enough."

Do I do that every time?

"Okay, even if that's true, it usually comes later in the process."

"Hmm. That's true. You're just getting started on this one." He studies his short nails like they're suddenly very interesting. "How's that going? The Cleary Oil thing?"

I wonder what he'd say if he knew I could see straight through him. "You mean, the fact that I'm seeing Paxton Cleary? It's going just fine."

"Has he tried to lasso you yet?"

"Oh, Matt." I shake my head. "Come on."

"That twang in his voice." He pretends to tip the brim of his invisible hat. *"Well, thank you, ma'am. I sure do hope you won't mind mah boots under your bed come mornin'."*

"Don't quit your day job."

He snorts. "Maybe he should quit his."

"What's that mean?" I pat Phoebe on the head, distracted now.

"Nothing." Again with the nails, which are perfectly clean from where I'm sitting.

"No way. You don't get to say that but not follow up with anything else."

He steals a look at me from the corner of his eye. "Cleary Oil has been unstable for months."

"Unstable?"

"There's been a lot of talk about them lately. The old man is, well, old. Not that there's anything wrong with that, but the board is starting to ask questions. Isn't it time for him to step down, all that."

"Hmm." I won't tell him about Paxton's concerns. It wouldn't be right. But it's interesting to know others are starting to hear whispers and rumors.

"All I'm saying is, I wouldn't invest in the company anytime soon. Not until they get this stuff worked out."

"Good thing I have no intention of investing." I can't help but study him closely, the way he's trying so hard to seem nonchalant. "Is there anything else you think I should know?"

"What else would there be?"

"Oh, for God's sake. Would you stop going around in circles?"

"I'm not trying to go around in circles."

"What are you trying to do then?"

"What's with the third degree?"

"I'm not trying to give you the third degree."

Phoebe's bark punctuates this and reminds me to cool off. She's clearly picking up on the mood in here and not liking it very much.

He blows out a long sigh. "Sorry. You have no idea how frustrating it is to have your every move second-guessed. Not just second-guessed, but the worst is always assumed. I only want to make sure you go into this with your eyes open."

"And I appreciate that," I start, speaking slowly and as kindly as I know how. "But here's what you need to remember. I'm only dating him—"

"For a book. What else is new?"

"Ew."

"It's the truth."

"You're right. It is the truth. I'm dating him because that's what I have to do."

"Bullshit."

"Don't talk to me that way."

"Stop deluding yourself then. You're not fooling me, so you must be trying to fool yourself."

"You're being disgusting, and I never invited you to come in and sit down. If all you want to do is start fights and be a jerk, you can go back across the hall."

We don't say anything for a while, and I console myself by getting down on the floor with Phoebe. She knows all about living with an obnoxious creep—poor thing.

"I'm not trying to start a fight," Matt eventually murmurs with a sigh. "I'm trying to protect you."

"I don't need you to do that."

"If you're trying to get into a relationship with this guy and you expect things to go smoothly, I just want you to know what you're getting into. There's a chance of the old man running the business into the ground, and the entire family could end up losing their money. You deserve to know that."

Is he right? It all lines up with what Paxton was already talking about last night.

Not that it matters. I have to get a little clarity on

this, and now's the only time to do it. If I don't get myself together now, I'll only end up falling harder for Paxton and earn myself a ton of grief.

"I don't want there to be anything more with him." It's not technically the truth, but I'll tell myself this as many times as necessary to get my head in the right place.

He shoots me a look that, if I'm trying to be nice, could be considered disbelieving.

"Why can't I just have fun? Why can't I enjoy my life? Isn't that what you and Hayley are always trying to convince me to do? Now, I'm having fun, and that's not good enough either. I wish you would make up your mind."

"If I thought you were the sort of person who could stay casual and have fun without getting emotionally wrapped up, I wouldn't care so much. I don't want you to get hurt. Or be disappointed. Isn't that what friends want for each other?"

When he talks that way, it's not easy to be mad at him. He always finds a way to get around me when he's the one who made me mad in the first place.

"I appreciate you caring," I tell Phoebe, meaning it for Matt. It's easier to say these things to him when I'm looking at her. Something about those deep brown puppy-dog eyes melts me. "And I'll be careful. I promise."

"What are you doing this weekend?"

The question is surprising enough to make me

forget the dog for a second and snap my head up to look at Matt. "Huh? Where'd that come from?"

"I'm going away for the weekend, and I was wondering if you'd watch her for me."

"Oh, sure."

"You don't think you'll have big plans?"

I roll my eyes. "Could you not be such a baby?"

"Who's being a baby?"

"You are. That was such a snarky way to ask."

"Well, don't you think you'll have plans?"

"No, I really don't." I can't help myself. "Where are you going?"

"Out of town for a couple of days. I have some things to do. Nothing to worry about."

Somehow, that doesn't make me feel much better. Clearly, there's still something bugging him. I know better than to push him too far. We'll only end up having the same argument all over again.

"You want to maybe order lunch in tomorrow?" I venture.

He offers the first genuine grin since coming in. "Sure. You buying?"

Chapter Ten

"YOU'VE GOT THIS." I adjust my boobs, using the old scoop-and-lift method before slipping a dress over my head and tying the belt around my waist. The reflection in the full-length mirror on the back of my bedroom door isn't half bad. Blue has always been my color. It brings out my eyes.

Everything's perfect—or it should be. It had better be, considering the trouble I've gone through today. Cleaning the apartment until I was ready to drop. I even made sure to stock condoms in the nightstand.

Hope springs eternal. Wouldn't want to get caught without them.

Dinner's due to be here around seven, which is when Paxton said he'd come around. He's been in meetings all day, and he seemed a little short via text. I can't help but think about what Matt told me. About the trouble the company's having.

Is that why they're in the city in the first place, he and his father? Why they're going to all these meetings? Who are they meeting with? Are they trying to sweet-talk the board?

And if they are, what business is it of mine?

I don't want to see Paxton's family fail, is all. But there isn't anything I can do about it either. I can be sensitive to his mood when he gets here though. And I can try to take his mind off it.

"Calm down," I whisper to myself after thinking this. Not like it's any use. My hormones have a mind of their own. And right now, the anxiety over having him here and making a nice night for us is nothing compared to the absolute frenzy my body goes into when I think about all the fun little ways to take his mind off work.

The food arrives on time. I decide to leave everything in the metal containers it came in, keeping it warm in the oven while waiting for my date.

And waiting.

It's seven thirty when I get a call.

"I'm on my way. I'm so sorry. The last meeting went way later than it was supposed to."

"That's okay." I mean, it is. It's perfectly fine. Are my insides all jumbled up? Did I just spend the past half hour questioning, oh, just about every decision I'd ever made? Like in my entire life?

But it's fine.

"I'll be there as soon as I can," he promises before ending the call.

This gives me a few minutes to freshen myself up since I spent the past half hour pacing and fidgeting with my hair.

Grandmother was right. Having it swept to the

side shows off my neck and shoulders. With age comes wisdom, I guess.

There's a knock at the door only a minute or so after I finish pulling the food from the oven.

"Hi, Paxton. Come on in," I say, greeting him at the door.

"Oh, it smells good," he says, pulling me into a tight hug and burying his face in my hair after stepping into my apartment. "You smell good too."

"Thank you. I can't take credit for the food. Sit down, make yourself comfortable."

"What a day." He loosens his tie, unbuttons the collar of his shirt, and then takes off his jacket.

The man knows how to wear a suit. No doubt about that.

Of course, I'd like to get him out of it—and fully intend to.

"Your meeting went so long. Is everything okay?" I'm busy plating the food but always with one eye on him. Wondering, wondering. Wishing Matt hadn't gotten into my head about Cleary Oil.

"Honestly, I don't even know."

That doesn't sound good, putting it mildly. "I'm sorry. Wine?"

"At least a bottle." He looks back over his shoulder with a smile. "Smells like Italian food."

"You're pretty quick on the uptake. I hope that's okay?"

"I'm so hungry; you'll be lucky to get any for yourself."

I bring the plates out to the coffee table since he's so comfortable on the couch. "Chicken Parmesan and a ton of pasta."

"Oh, that's miraculous."

He's already digging in by the time I bring back a couple of glasses of wine.

"I hope you don't think I'm rude, but I had a light lunch." He looks me up and down while chewing. "Now that I'm eating and I can think straight, you look fantastic."

"Thank you." I'm still so nervous; I can barely bring myself to eat. It feels like my first date.

Is this what it's supposed to feel like when things are for real? When there's more to a potential relationship than fooling around, having fun?

Or am I kidding myself?

He wolfs down one chicken breast and then starts on the second a little more slowly. "So, tell me about your day. Remind me there are people in the world who live normal lives."

"I don't know how many people would call my life normal," I admit with a chuckle. The wine helps loosen me up some, which is just what I need. Otherwise, I'll sweat through the dress. Not the sexiest look.

He glances around the apartment, taking everything in. "I didn't get much of a look the other night. I was busy making sure that neighbor didn't bite my head off."

"What do you think?" Why does he have to

bring up Matt? He's the last person I want to think about right now. Bad enough that I can't stop fretting over Paxton's company, thanks to his little bit of advice.

"I think it's beautiful." He gestures to the bookshelves. "I love the way you have them arranged by color. Very smart. At least you have plenty of space to work out of."

"True. I like working right by the window, over there." I nod to the table that serves as a desk, positioned between the two big windows looking out over the street.

"I imagine there's plenty to inspire you out there."

"And distract me, if I'm not careful."

"I know I said it before, but it bears repeating." He wipes his mouth with a napkin before settling back with his wine. "I give you all the credit in the world for being self-driven. It must take a lot of discipline to finish a book. Especially at the rate you've been publishing."

I turn away from my food to face him. "Uh, how do you know that? I didn't tell you anything about publishing so rapidly now." My knee nudges his. "You've been researching again."

His already-tan skin seems to darken a little. Wow, to think, I can make a man like him blush. "Sometimes, I have a hard time falling asleep at night in a strange place. Like my hotel room, you know. I've done a little reading these last couple of nights."

I rub my hands over my thighs to dry the nervous sweat that magically slicked them when he said that. "Why is it one thing for hundreds of strangers to read my work and another thing for just one person?"

"Because you know me and I'm sitting right here in front of you?"

"Yeah, that could have something to do with it." I need the rest of my wine, so I drink it and wonder if I should have another glass. Or two.

"Would you relax?" He lifts one of my hands to his lips and gently kisses it. "You're a terrific writer. Seriously. I couldn't stop turning the pages."

"You mean that?" I croak in disbelief.

"Yes, ma'am, I surely do. And when it came to the hot scenes?" He blows out a long whistle. "I've gotta hand it to your imagination. Unless all those things actually happened …"

He gets a tiny smack for that.

"Not that it's any of your business, but I made almost all of that up. The situations were inspired by real life, but most of the sex came from up here." I tap my head.

"Most of it?"

"You want specific examples?"

"No, not necessarily. Just curious how much of our time together will be read by thousands of people."

"You worried I won't do you justice?"

"I don't worry about that. I worry your editor will think you're handing her erotica instead of your usual romance."

I shouldn't laugh. The situation is way too serious. Too sexy, too full of promise. I manage to hold most of it back—only a snicker squeaks out. "Believe me, she wouldn't think that was a problem."

He lifts an eyebrow. "Challenge accepted."

We're both too stuffed right now to even think about that though. It doesn't need to be said. I slip off my shoes, and he takes his off at my urging.

"I can't lie, those shoes start to hurt once you've been wearing them all day. I'm much more comfortable in a pair of boots."

"I would like to see you out there, on the ranch, in your natural element."

"I would like you to see me there." His fingers find mine, winding around them. "That's where I feel most myself. Not in a boardroom or an office. Out on the land, training horses."

"What's that like?"

"You have to get the horse to trust you, and then it takes patience. We like to start with young horses, around age two. We have to teach them the lead changes and riding cues. It's usually best to start racing them at five."

"Racing? I thought they just bucked?"

"Oh, sorry, I wasn't clear before. I train them for barrel racing. We have to condition them like one would an athlete. It's tough on them, so we take our time and make sure they're ready."

"Wow, it's amazing to think of them as athletes."

"Yes. And when I have to go into the office, I have to hand the training over to my mentor. I miss seeing the progress the horses make while I'm away."

"I bet. You know, I've never been to a rodeo."

"Never?" he asks incredulously.

I shake my head. "Maybe I can attend one sometime," I hint.

"When you come to Texas, I'll make sure you get to see one."

"So, do you ever have to swing a lasso?" I pretend to do that, swinging my arm over my head. Gently since I'm still holding wine in that hand. The other one is clasping his, and I wouldn't trade that for anything.

"Sometimes. If a horse gets out of line."

"Oh, and what would you do to me if I got out of line?" I flirt, setting my wine down.

"Oh, I can think of a few things I could do with some rope to keep you just where I needed you."

We're both smiling as we lean in for a kiss, which quickly turns into more. We're not out in the hall this time. We're not on a park bench.

And I'm not wearing pants like I was last night.

His hand runs up my thigh while his tongue plunges into my mouth. I don't mind either. In fact,

I wrap my leg around his to draw him closer, to show him I want more.

"What was that you were saying about a challenge accepted?" I manage before gasping when his fingertips graze the hem of my panties.

He's laughing as he lifts me straight up off the couch with no effort. There is something so insanely sexy about being so easily handled, knowing he's strong enough to pick me up and carry me off.

In this case, he's carrying me off to the bedroom, my legs wrapped around him, and I don't know if I'm going to be able to let go.

Chapter Eleven

AMAZING, WHAT A good lay will do for a girl's outlook.

Is it just me, or is the sun a little brighter today? Are the birds singing a little louder? Is their song sweeter? The morning after Paxton's visit, I might as well be a cartoon princess, floating through the apartment. If a cheerful squirrel randomly came in through the window to help me with the chores, I wouldn't be surprised.

Nothing can stop me today. Even my writing flows smoothly, thanks to the inspiration Paxton provided last night.

Repeatedly.

The man is healthy; I'll give him that. Maybe there's something in the water down in Texas, or maybe it's all that hard work he's put in over the years. His body is used to working for hours on end, on the rigs. A little thing like sex must seem like a vacation in comparison.

Though the sex was no little thing. He's no little thing either. I can't help but laugh to myself when I imagine what Maggie would have to say if I were crude and trashy enough to describe him in detail.

I might have to share that kind of in-depth information with Hayley, and she's about the only person in the world I would ever consider gossiping with like that.

When noon rolls around, I'm almost proud of myself for having remembered my lunch date with Matt. Granted, I'm not completely sure it's a good idea for us to get together today—he was still acting sort of funny when he was over here last—but it's not like our relationship hasn't hit bumps before.

"I'm starting to think you offered to buy lunch today for an excuse to hang out with the dog." He doesn't sound disapproving when he makes this observation.

"You know me too well."

He grins at Phoebe, who's sitting between us and looking hopeful. "So, how did it go last night?"

And there it is. Why does he have to do this? If I were a dog like Phoebe, my hackles would go up at the mere mention of last night because I know what he's really driving at. He wants details. He wants to tease and torment me.

And then there's the fact that I get the feeling he doesn't like Paxton very much, though I'm not sure why. Is there something he's not telling me? Would that be such a surprise? Frankly, no matter how well we've gotten to know each other, there are still many mysteries surrounding my neighbor that I haven't come close to cracking yet.

JILLIAN DODD

With a smile, I ask, "What happened last night? Why would you ask that?"

He digs around with his chopsticks, snickering. "Oh, so that's how we're going to play it."

"Play what? Who's playing?"

"You know as well as I do that I could hear his voice from my apartment. Remember, thin walls?"

Ugh, I can never hide anything from him.

He cocks an eyebrow. "So? How did it go?"

Part of me wants to lash out, to tell him he knows damn well how it went if he could hear so clearly from across the hall. I tried as hard as I could to keep things quiet, and for the most part, I succeeded. But there are times when a girl can't contain herself, and one of those times is when she's in the throes of passion.

Considering Paxton brought me to that point three times last night, Matt was bound to hear something.

"I could boink every night for the next year and scream like a banshee the entire time, and it wouldn't come anywhere close to what I've heard coming from your apartment."

"So, there was boinking. I see." He snorts a little, going for another dumpling.

"Why not? We're dating."

"So, is it true what they say?"

I shouldn't ask. I shouldn't even entertain him. "Is what true?" I ask against my better judgment.

"Is everything bigger in Texas?"

"You are such a pig!" But I can't help the way my cheeks flush. It's a sensation that spreads down my throat and to my chest.

"I'll take that as a yes." He laughs at my reaction. "Lighten up. It's not such a big deal."

"Then, why did you bring it up?"

"Don't you know by now how I love to see you squirm?"

I look at Phoebe, who looks at me with her soulful doggy eyes. "Seriously, how do you put up with him?"

"So, how much longer is Prince Charming going to be in town?"

"He'll go home this weekend."

"So, I guess that would be the end of that. I hope you got enough information for your book."

I glance up from my tofu and vegetables with a shrug. "Actually, he mentioned something about having me come out to visit him next week."

"Oh, really?" There's a flatness in his voice now. He's not wearing that shit-eating grin anymore.

"Don't worry; I'll still be here to watch Phoebe. I already told him I have responsibilities this weekend."

"It's very generous of him to allow you to help a friend in need."

"Considering I'm the writer, you have a way of being overly dramatic about things that even I don't understand. And that's saying something." When he doesn't fire back a snarky response, I add, "Is there something you're not telling me? Something about him? Do you know more about his situation that I don't?"

"You're just going to get mad at me."

"That's a great start. I hope you know you'd better keep going, or you'll get a chopstick through the eye."

"Rumors make their way around." He shrugs. "I don't pay attention to most of what I hear. By the time I hear gossip about these heavy hitters, it's usually already been passed through five or six different people. Like one long game of telephone. By the time news gets to me, there's no telling how much of it is completely made up."

"What did you hear? Seriously, tell me. I will lock you in this apartment until you do."

"You do realize, there are worse things in life, right? I mean, it's a pretty comfortable apartment."

"You don't think I could make your life miserable if I put my mind to it?"

He winces. "Fair enough. It's just that I remember reading in some news item a few months ago that he was seriously involved with the daughter of some big oil tycoon down in Texas."

"I was dating someone a while ago. So what?"

"I'm talking, merger potential. Both business and personal." He lowers his brow, eyes boring into me. "You know what I'm saying."

"He was engaged?"

"I don't know for sure really."

"Then, why even bring it up if you don't know? Why would I care about what he was doing a few months ago? Unless he was serving time for murder or something like that, it's none of my business. We're only casually seeing each other."

"Give me a break, Valentine. I heard you over here today, singing to yourself. All happy and stuff. When I came in, you were smiling for no reason. And now, your shoulders are up around your ears, and you're defensive and upset."

Why is it making me so uncomfortable, having this conversation with him? We usually discuss just about everything under the sun, and it almost never bothers me. But this? Maybe because it feels like an invasion of privacy.

Maybe because I don't want to hear what he has to say about Paxton.

"That's where the gossip comes in," he continues. When he puts his food aside, I know he's serious, so for the sake of not getting in a fight, I put my food aside as well and face him head-on. "Rumor had it at the time that he was dating this girl and thinking about getting married for himself and for the business. That's where the merger part comes in."

"So, what you're saying is, he's only interested in a relationship with somebody who's going to help save his company down the line?"

"That's the long and short of it. Hey, don't shoot the messenger." He holds his hands up in surrender. "That's the way it goes for some of these businesses. These wealthy tycoons, they have to protect what's theirs, and if there's trouble or the potential for it down the line, they'll do what they can to lessen the damage."

Darn it.

Why does he have to do this?

Why does he have to make me unhappy?

I was flying high earlier; my heart had wings. I haven't been able to stop thinking about last night—the heat, the tenderness, and the mind-blowing, toe-curling pleasure. He worshipped me, cherished me. We connected more deeply than I have with a man in just about as long as I can remember.

When the stinging starts behind my eyes, I know I'm in big trouble. Which is why I get up, go to the kitchen, and rummage around in the fridge like I'm looking for something. Really, I don't want him to see me cry.

"You're upset," he announces from his place on the couch.

"No, I'm not."

"Then, why are you standing there with your head in the fridge and your back turned to me?"

"You know, there are times when I'm pretty sure you get off on upsetting me. And it's not enough to upset me, but you have to pick at it." I probably slam the refrigerator door harder than necessary, but now, I'm mad. On the verge of furious in fact.

He has the nerve to look surprised, even offended. "I'm trying to be your friend!"

"No, you can't stand to see me happy for even two minutes of my life. After everything I've gone through in this freaking experiment Maggie insisted I start with—much of which you've been aware of—I finally feel good. I feel like this could be right. This could go someplace. So, naturally, you have to come in with a big, sharp pin and stick it in my balloon. Do you take pleasure in this?"

"I should've known." He gets his things together, closing up half-full containers and stacking them to take back to his apartment. "Some people can't be helped."

"Oh, you're such a sweet person," I snap. "What a generous guy you are. What a saint."

"You're being nasty and childish."

"And you're obsessed with my personal life because yours has gone down the tubes!"

I know the second it's out of my mouth that it was the wrong thing to say. Sure, it felt good, coming out, but I regret it instantly.

His face scrunches up a little, like he's recovering from a blow. "So, that's what you think this is about?" he whispers.

"Well? What else? You used to bring home a new girl almost every night. You used to go out; you had a social life. Now, you're a homebody, and you got annoyed with me because I had something to do on Sunday night. I'm sorry if I can't arrange my schedule around your lack of a social life."

Kitty, what is wrong with you? Where is this coming from?

I can't seem to keep my mouth shut. I don't even believe half of what I'm saying, but he's hurt me so much, left me feeling hopeless and inadequate. Not to mention hopelessly naive, like a real idiot for ever thinking Paxton might get serious about me.

He shakes his head with a sad little smile. "You know, you're one of the smartest people I know. I give you a lot of shit; I realize that. I tease you; I joke around. But really, your intelligence has impressed me on more than one occasion."

I should be kind, shouldn't I? I should extend an olive branch.

Instead, I double down out of a stupid sense of self-preservation. "Um, thanks? What's that got to do with anything?"

"You just don't get it. You still don't see. I'm starting to think you never will. Because you don't want to. I guess I need to get a grip once and for all." With that, he picks up the rest of his food and motions for Phoebe to follow him back to their place.

I trot behind them. "Wait a second! I'm not finished yet."

"Too bad because I am."

He tries to close the apartment door before I can get through, but he's too late. I manage to shove my way in and follow him to the kitchen.

"If there's something I need to get, as you put it, why won't you come right out and tell me? What's with all this secrecy? Since when do you not tell it like it is?"

"Some things can't be said so easily." Now, it's his turn to go to the fridge, like I'm not even here.

"Can't you just talk to me? What is going on? I'm sorry for being nasty before. Don't shut me out, please."

He barks out a bitter laugh before closing the refrigerator door and turning to me. The expression on his face makes me fall back a step. It's something between anger and … desperation? Frustration?

"You think saying you're sorry erases what you just said? Like I'm going to forget? It doesn't work that way. Trust me, if it did, my life would be a lot simpler right now."

"Meaning what?"

He tries to turn away, and I give him a little shove to hold his attention.

"Don't turn your back on me! Tell me what it is. What is so hard about your life right now? What haven't you told me?"

He looks at the floor. "Don't do this. I'm serious. Just go home."

"Why won't you talk to me?"

His eyes lift, darting over my face before narrowing. "Fine. You want me to talk to you? I'll talk to you. You live in this little bubble. You only see what you want to see; you only hear what you feel like hearing. And maybe that's my fault. In fact, I know a lot of it is my fault."

"You're not making any sense."

"What else is new? You don't give any thought to how you might affect other people. Or how, sometimes, being in your corner is more trouble than it's worth."

"Is that how you feel right now? That I'm more trouble than I'm worth?"

"Right now? Hell yeah. My life was a lot simpler before you drunkenly stumbled over here one night and asked me how to write a sex scene."

I take a step back, flabbergasted. "Well, if I'm such a problem for you, don't let me screw up your life anymore. But don't get pissy with me when we can't get together on a Sunday night either."

He snorts. The disdain written on his face is striking, disheartening. "Are you blind? Or are you willfully ignorant? I'm trying to tell you something here, and you're not listening."

"Then, just come out and say it because I'm no closer to understanding you than I was before!"

He doesn't say it.

Instead, he does something I wouldn't have anticipated in a million years.

He reaches out.

Takes me by the arms.

Pulls me to him before I even know what's happening.

And he kisses me.

My body goes stiff in surprise, total shock. It's not a sweet kiss. Not tender. It's hard. Fierce. But no less passionate. I don't have time to register what's happening, how I should react, before he pulls away.

"Does that answer your question?" He lets me go and turns away again, breathing heavy. "Seriously, you should go. I shouldn't have done that. This has gotten out of hand. It would be best—"

I don't need to hear any more. I don't want to either. Because I have absolutely no idea what the hell just happened. I'm out the door before he has a chance to finish his sentence.

Chapter Twelve

"AND THAT'S IT. I texted you, like, two seconds later. And then I buried myself under my blankets for most of the afternoon because I didn't know how to deal with it."

Hayley sits across from me, sipping her drink with an air of nonchalance that I find truly disturbing.

I wave a hand in front of her face. "Hello? Did you hear anything I just said? Matt kissed me. Matt! Of all people! Help me figure this out because I am lost."

She tips her head to the side. "Are you though?"

"What?"

"You're seriously lost? It comes as such a massive shock that Matt kissed you?"

"Okay, did I stumble into a parallel universe? Because nothing is making any sense right now. Why would I not be surprised? He's practically my brother."

My beautiful, brilliant best friend lowers her glass to the table with a sigh before reaching across and taking my hand. "Kitty, I'm telling you this with all the love in my heart. You are completely delusional when you set your mind to it."

"Wow, and that was said with love? I would hate to hear it if it wasn't."

"Be a smart-ass all you want; that doesn't change anything." She has to let go of me when our server brings a plate of nachos.

"Your extra side of guacamole and one of extra cheese," he murmurs, placing the pair of ramekins beside the platter.

If nothing else, this is a situation that requires extra cheese and guacamole.

Even the sight and smell of the nachos doesn't dissuade me from what's going on. "I don't understand."

She rolls her eyes. "Kitty, when are you going to wake up and figure out that he's in love with you?"

My head snaps back hard enough that I'm afraid I might have whiplash.

She only picks up her drink again, and with the other hand, she pulls a large chip loaded with chicken and cheese from the pile between us. "Act as surprised as you want, but somebody has to tell you eventually. He's crazy about you. And maybe you honestly haven't seen it. I'm not trying to call you ignorant or anything like that. Maybe you truly didn't know. But it's plain to me that he's had feelings for you for a long time. Just looking at the two of you together makes it pretty clear to me."

I'm so stunned; I can barely speak.

Matt? Matt Ryder from across the hall? In love with me? Why is the room suddenly spinning?

My every impulse tells me to refute this. To shake my head and fold my arms and refuse to listen.

But that wouldn't get me anywhere. Besides, I genuinely want to understand. I really do.

"I've only ever considered us close friends," I murmur before picking at the chips.

"That doesn't mean he hasn't seen things in a different way. Lots of close friendships end up turning into something more, you know."

"We're so different. There hasn't ever been anything like this between us before. Like, I never got the idea he even liked me a little, much less anything else."

"With all due respect, I feel like you didn't want to see it."

I don't know what to think. Even the nachos don't taste as good as usual, which is somehow the straw that comes close to breaking the camel's back. I want to cry.

"What are you so upset about?" Hayley pats my arm. "It's nothing to cry over, but you look like you're ready to weep."

"I said really awful things to him," I manage with a tremor in my voice. "If he has those feelings for me, I probably hurt him pretty badly. I didn't mean to do that."

"I'm sure you didn't."

That isn't all. I wish I could make sense of the storm whipping around in my head. "I don't want things to change. I like things the way they are. It's too complicated, the idea of being with somebody who lives right there across the hall. What if things didn't work out? I wouldn't be able to get away from him. I mean, for God's sake, I can barely handle embarrassing myself in front of him. What if we were together and we broke up?"

"You're really thinking this through, aren't you? I think you might be getting ahead of yourself."

"You're the one who just said he's in love with me. How am I supposed to live across the hall from him, knowing how he feels? When I don't feel the same way?"

She dips her chin, staring at me with a very serious look. "You're my best friend. I know you better than just about anybody in the world knows you. So, excuse me if I don't believe that."

I shake my head hard enough to make my ponytail swing back and forth violently. "No. Don't put thoughts in my head that aren't there. Don't trick me into falling for him."

"I'm not trying to do any such thing!"

"But you are. I'm telling you how I feel. Who would know better than I do about how I feel about him? It's not fair for you to come back at me and insist I feel differently than I do. You're planting ideas in my head, and that sort of thing only ever ends badly."

She grumbles but eventually sighs. "Okay. You're allowed to feel how you feel."

"I don't know what to do. I don't want things to be weird for us."

"I hate to tell you, but they're going to be weird now. For a little while at least."

"Terrific." Shoving a bunch of nachos in my face doesn't make me feel much better.

"You might need to give him space. But I'm sure he'll get over it."

"You don't think we should talk it over? I mean, I'm all about avoiding uncomfortable situations whenever possible, but is this the kind of thing that can be ignored? And if I do ignore it or pretend like nothing out of the ordinary happened, would that be insulting? I don't want him thinking I don't care about his feelings. I might not like him that way, but I don't want to hurt him. Even if he drives me nuts, he's still a good friend. I guess I started counting on him more than I knew."

"I guess you did. He sort of snuck up on you, didn't he?"

"Yeah. I hate thinking he's unhappy because of me."

"Well, if he does have these feelings for you, I can imagine it would be difficult to watch you date different people."

"Oh God, this is making me feel even worse."

"I'm not trying to make you feel worse. I'm try-ing to figure it out." She rests her chin on her palm while picking at the nachos. "No wonder he's been a little testy."

"I wish he had come out and been honest with me earlier."

"What good would that have done? It would have just made you second-guess yourself all this time."

"I guess that's true." Then, I slap a palm to my forehead. "I'm supposed to be watching Phoebe this weekend too. So, it's not like I can completely avoid him."

"Then again, that could be the reason for the two of you to see each other again and maybe talk things out."

"Oh, sure. I can imagine how well that will go. Honestly, I shudder to think."

She shrugs. "Hey, what's the alternative? Avoiding him until one of you moves out? That's not going to work either."

"Stop being right all the time."

"I can't help it. That's just the way it usually turns out." She signals for another round of drinks without asking if I'm interested or not. She knows me too well.

Though I suspect no amount of alcohol is going to make up for my complete confusion and lack of direction on this.

"What about your cowboy?" she asks, and I would kiss her if I were so inclined. I've already done enough to embarrass myself in this place though, so I stay put and keep my lips to myself.

Lips Matt kissed earlier.

Dammit, I have to stop thinking about it.

"My cowboy? As far as I know, he's busy to-night. Business stuff. But he was certainly feeling okay last night." Right now, I will talk about anything so long as it turns focus away from how uncomfortable my life has become.

She practically climbs over the table in anticipation. "Spill! I've been dying all day to know what happened."

"You mean, what happened three times?" I hold up three fingers in case her hearing suddenly failed.

She fans herself. "Oh, I so hate you."

We are well into our drinks and almost finished with the nachos when my phone buzzes. My heart skips a beat when I see it's Paxton who texted.

Just got out of my meeting, and I'm dying to see you.

"Is that him? What did he say?" She then falls back a little, grinning. "Unless it's too spicy for me to know about."

"Sorry to disappoint you, but it's not spicy. He wants to see me."

What's that fluttering in my stomach? Granted, it could be the combination of martinis and nachos, but I would like to think it has more to do with anticipation. We didn't exactly make plans to get together tonight, but that doesn't mean I wasn't hoping he would reach out once his work was done for the day.

"Are you going to his hotel?"

I look up from the screen, where I was about to invite him over, frowning. "I don't know. I was going to ask him to come to my place."

She winces, shaking her head. "Bad idea."

For the second time, I slap my forehead. "I am entirely too tipsy to make good decisions right now. Of course, it would be a terrible idea to have him come over tonight."

I chew my lip, looking down at the phone. "But I don't want to be obvious about it either. I don't want to invite myself to his hotel."

"Be flirtatious about it. Tell him you'll show up, wearing a raincoat and nothing else."

"That's a little heavier than flirtation."

"It'll get the desired results, won't it? Unless you think he would turn you down."

"He'd damn well better not." I chuckle. Of course, now, she has me wondering. "Maybe I should tell him the truth?"

She waves her hands around. "No way! Jeez, for a romance writer, you're clueless about emotions."

"Gee, thanks a lot."

"You can't tell him about Matt. That would just make things more awkward."

"Of course."

We both look at the phone when it buzzes with a new text.

I'm going to freshen up and grab something to eat. Want to come by?

"See? No worries." Hayley sits back with a smug smile, like she had anything to do with what just happened. Like she somehow mentally sent a message to Paxton, who she has never met, advising him to have me over for a booty call.

"No worries," I echo, polishing off my drink.

And that might be true, too, if only I could stop worrying about Matt and his feelings. Of all the times for him to decide he has feelings for me.

Of all the times for me to wonder how many signals I missed along the way.

Chapter Thirteen

CONTRARY TO HAYLEY'S opinion, I'm wearing normal street clothes by the time I walk into the lobby of The Plaza Hotel. I'm all about making memories and everything, but there are limits.

Though she did give me an idea for my book, and goodness knows, Maggie would love a scene like that.

But this is real life, and it's my heart that's really thudding as I look around the lobby. He told me he would meet me here rather than have me go to his room by myself. I got the feeling he was afraid the front-desk staff would think I was a professional, somebody the wealthy cowboy had called in for the night.

Expect he's not here. The man sticks out like a sore thumb. There's no missing him. Yet there's no sign of him in the lobby with its intricate floor and magnificent chandelier hanging in front of the elevators. This has always seemed like such a magical place, like a fairy-tale land.

Right now, I feel like an intruder. Like some-body's going to know just by looking at me that I'm not staying here and only here to hook up with a guest. I'm a grown woman. Why does that bother me so much? I'll never see any of these people again.

It's not like any of them could possibly know I already kissed another man today—rather, that I was kissed by another man.

Yikes. I can't get over the feeling that I should tell Paxton, but it really isn't any of his business, is it? We're not even seriously dating. I would never call him my boyfriend, not yet anyway. For all I know, he could've made out with another girl today.

Terrific. Now, I'm imagining that, and it's not doing me any favors.

Rather than stand around, feeling like I don't belong, I wander toward the lounge with its circular bar. The skylight above the bar is made entirely of stained glass and is gorgeous enough to take my breath away.

There's another gorgeous thing sitting underneath the intricate glass ceiling. He's on his phone with a tumbler of whiskey in front of him, and he does not look happy.

I take a minute to watch him, to stand back without him knowing I'm here. He turns the glass around and around, scowling at it like it did something to offend him.

Who could he be talking to? Isn't his father staying here in the hotel with him?

He heaves a sigh that makes me remember the rise and fall of his shoulders when he got off the phone a few nights ago while we were in the park. This is a far cry from the genial, charming man I've been spending time with.

"Can I help you, miss?" The bartender waits expectantly in front of me. He raised his voice a little louder than he needed to, like he's trying to send a message. *Buy a drink or get out of here.*

It's enough to get Paxton's attention, and he's suddenly smiling. The difference is so sudden, so complete. Within seconds, he's off the phone, waving me over. I give the bartender a look and make my way over to Paxton.

"I didn't know you were there," he says as I approach the table.

"I didn't want to disturb you while you were on the phone."

"You're so sweet." He nods to his glass. "Would you like a drink?"

"No, thanks. I met up with my best friend earlier, and we had drinks."

"That's Hayley, right?"

"Yep. The genius lawyer who will probably be the youngest partner her firm has ever seen."

"Good for her. And she still has time to have a drink with her friend. She's better at balancing work and her personal life than I'll ever be." With that, he finishes his drink all at once before signing the slip, which the bartender discreetly left in front of him.

He stands, wrapping me in a chaste hug. "You have no idea how much I want to tear your clothes off right now," he growls in my ear.

I bite my lip and try to give him as coy of a look as I can. "But, Mr. Cleary, what would everyone in the bar think?"

"They'd think I'd found the most beautiful, most interesting, sexiest woman in the world. I don't think anybody would blame me."

I have to fight the impulse to correct him. Why is it so hard for me to accept a compliment? Why do I immediately want to shut him down and tell him he's absolutely crazy for being attracted to me? Where does that start, I wonder?

He's clearly not worried about it, draping an arm over my shoulders and leading me out of the lounge and toward the elevators. "How was your day?" he asks as we walk.

Oh boy. There's no way he could possibly know what a loaded question that is. For a split second, I almost want to tell him that my day was insane enough to warrant a 911 text to my bestie, begging her to meet me for drinks before I lost my sanity.

"Pretty good," I settle on replying.

He surprises me by frowning at this. "Just *pretty good*? Maybe I didn't do all I could last night ..."

I can't help but giggle, ducking my head a little as I do. "Trust me, I don't know what else you could have done."

"Ma'am, there's always room for improvement."

The elevator doors open, and we step into the empty car.

Paxton takes advantage of this. The second the doors close, his hands are on me, his mouth covering mine. He kisses me like a man who's starving, desperate for me.

If there's anything sexier in the entire world, I don't know what it is. And while I've always heard the threat of being discovered only makes a situation like this sexier, I've never known from personal experience just how true it is.

Now, I do. Now, I understand. Here we are, in this swanky hotel, with Paxton pushing me up against the wall and one of his hands up under my blouse. If the car came to a stop, we might have time to fix ourselves up before the doors opened, but it would be a close call. And there's no way whoever joined us wouldn't know what was going on before they showed up.

We barely make it to his room before clothes start coming off.

"THAT'S PEPPERMINT." PAXTON hands me his phone to show me a picture of the most beautiful collie I've ever seen, sitting pretty on a patch of emerald grass.

"Oh, she's adorable!"

His smile has all the pride of a parent. "I've raised her since she was a pup. She's a great companion." That smile turns to a sheepish grin as he rolls onto his back. "Is it wrong that I always look at a picture of her at night before I go to sleep?"

My heart just about melts before I lean over to kiss him. "I think that's the sweetest thing I've ever heard."

He strains upward to kiss me again. "If you think that's sweet, I have lots of stories to tell you. So long as I get a reward after each one."

"You're incorrigible." I climb out of bed with a sheet wrapped around me and grab a bottle of water from the minibar. He holds his hand out, silently requesting one for himself, so I grab a second bottle before returning to the bed.

"Are you serious about wanting to come out and visit?" he asks.

"Are you serious about wanting me to come out?"

"Most definitely." There's a new light in his eyes when he says it too. Genuine enthusiasm—at least, that's what I want it to be. Like he really, truly wants me to visit and learn about the things he loves. Including Peppermint, his loyal dog.

"Then, I'm serious about coming to visit. Just for the purpose of research, of course."

"Of course. As per our original agreement." He winks before lifting the water to his lips. If ever a man deserved a water break, it's this one.

Wouldn't Maggie have a fit if she knew how sore I was? The woman would never shut up about it. I sincerely wish the thought of her didn't come to mind in a moment like this. There's nothing as unsexy as thinking about one's editor while recuperating from a roll in the sheets.

Paxton's suite is now littered with our clothes, the trail leading from the front door, through the sitting area, and into the bedroom. I can't help but feel a little smug, and I wonder if there's a girl in the world who wouldn't. Here I am, in bed with an absolutely gorgeous, incredible man who could have any woman he wanted. I'm the one whose clothes he tore off the second we were in the door.

"I could send the jet out for you as early as Monday, if you want. I'll be getting in on Sunday, so that should give the help enough time to make sure there's a room prepared for you at the house."

"Tell me about your house," I urge. "You made it sound like you live close to your family."

"We all live on the ranch in our own separate houses."

"Really? So, what, are you all on top of each other?"

I can tell he tries not to laugh, but he isn't very successful. "I can go an entire week without seeing my daddy or my brothers."

"Wow. Just how much land are we talking about here?"

"Roughly four hundred thousand acres." Now, he laughs for real. "Seems like I keep surprising you."

"I'm sorry, but I can't even imagine how big that must be."

"You have to see it for yourself. I can describe it all I want, but there's nothing like seeing it with your own eyes." He inches over, taking hold of my chin to turn my face toward him. "Beautiful eyes, by the way."

Help me; I'm about to swoon. "It looks like I have no choice but to visit then."

"It does look that way."

"Are we going to visit the rest of your family? No, probably not," I decide. "I'm sure they'll all be too busy."

"I'm sure they will be." He gets out of bed, not bothering to wrap himself up like I did, and makes his way to the spot where his pants came off. He pulls them back on and sits back on the bed before he starts scrolling through his phone again.

Great. I said something wrong. "I'm sorry. Should I not have brought up your family? I'm not trying to—"

He smiles, shaking his head, though he still strikes me as being rather distracted all of a sudden. "No, it's just that you got me thinking. I want to be sure right now, while you're on my mind, to remind my father and my brothers to give me some alone time next week when you're visiting. I want you all to myself."

Well, there's no universe in which I wouldn't find that flattering. And the thought of being with him and only him on that big ranch with all the horses and Peppermint and the big, wide-open spaces is sort of thrilling.

Even if I get a sneaking suspicion he expects me to ride a horse, which I have never done.

He laughs in surprise when I tell him this. "Are you serious?"

"How can you doubt it?" When he sputters in amazement, I remind him, "I didn't grow up in this world. I grew up in Brooklyn. I'm sure lots of girls my age, whose grandparents were wealthy, took horse-riding lessons or whatever, but that's not how I grew up. My mom wanted to keep me away from that life."

"Of course. It would be like you laughing if I told you I'd never ridden a subway."

"You do realize, we're going to have to do that before you leave, right? Just so you can say you have?"

Instead of blanching or patting me on the head and calling me naive, he growls and pounces on me. "If it's all the same to you, ma'am, I would rather ride something else."

Who am I to argue with that logic?

Chapter Fourteen

I FEEL LIKE a teenager, sneaking in after breaking curfew.

Only I haven't been a teenager in years.

And no one sets a curfew for me anymore.

And it's my apartment building I'm sneaking into.

So, why the heck am I practically tiptoeing down the hall Friday morning? Because a certain somebody who lives across the hall works early in the morning—that's why. I know if I'm not careful, he'll hear me, and he might be compelled to come out and confront me.

Maybe *confront* is too strong a word. At least, I hope it is. I hope he doesn't feel enough negativity toward me to want a confrontation while I'm wearing last night's clothes.

Everything seems quiet while I creep along with my shoes in one hand. The term *walk of shame* comes to mind. Why should it? I have nothing to be ashamed of. I spent a night at The Plaza with a man who excites me at the very thought of him. If anything, I should take out a full-page ad in the

Times and gloat about my good fortune.

There isn't any light coming from under Matt's door, which strikes me as odd. It's a little past six in the morning, meaning he should have been up a while ago to check the overseas markets' overnight developments. It's still dark enough outside that a light would be a good idea, but he doesn't have one on.

Terrific. Am I going to worry about him nonstop now, all because I know he has feelings for me? Does it make me a bad person to even have that thought in the first place? He's not a burden. And it isn't his fault.

There's a note at my feet when I open the door to my place. He must've slid it under. *Decided to leave early. Phoebe is fed and walked for the morning. Be back Sunday night.*

I don't know whether this is a relief or something else to worry about. I guess I should stick to relief and leave it there. I don't have to face him this morning—a meeting I've been dreading ever since remembering his request to watch the dog for the weekend.

I just wish it didn't feel so much like something was broken that couldn't be fixed.

Before going across the hall to grab the dog—it makes sense to have her with me, in my apartment, rather than keeping her cooped up by herself and only checking on her occasionally—I change into my yoga clothes and unroll my mat in front of the window. It's a little early for me, to say the least, since I work until the early morning hours.

Yoga is normally the last thing on my mind at this time of morning. I'm usually in dreamland.

Frankly, I could use a little extra time in dreamland after spending most of the night awake with Paxton. Not that I'm complaining.

By the time I finish my practice and take a shower, the sun is fully up and flooding my apartment with brilliant light. I can't help but take that as a sign of good things to come. Reasons to be happy.

And having Phoebe as a companion all weekend isn't such a bad thought. She won't look at me with resentment or bitterness, like her owner probably would right now.

"I'LL FLY OUT to the ranch on Monday, and I can't wait." Am I grinning like a goofball? Probably. I can't help myself.

"My, that is exciting. I've always wanted to see one of those large outfits for myself. Though the thought of the smell doesn't exactly thrill me." My grandmother wrinkles her patrician nose, like she can already smell the horses. And what comes out of them.

"I was thinking the same thing! I guess it's the sort of thing you get used to. But shouldn't most of it be in the barn? Maybe I can avoid that area."

"Be careful out there. I wouldn't want to find out you'd been trampled."

"I hardly think Paxton would put me in a position where I might get trampled. The horses sound well-trained."

"Animals are unpredictable, my dear. One never knows what's going on in their heads. They don't know their own size or strength either, especially when compared to a small girl such as yourself."

I would hardly call myself small. "I'll make sure to warn him that he'll have you to deal with if anything like that happens."

"Do that." She sets down her cup and saucer with a tiny frown. "Something's bothering you."

"Huh?" My smile widens as I become self-conscious. "I'm super excited about seeing the ranch and writing about it. And Paxton's great. Things are going better with him than with any of the others I've dated."

"Mmhmm. Which is why it strikes me as odd that you're looking so distressed."

Darn that grandmotherly intuition of hers. Am I wearing a sign around my neck or something? Maybe it's written across my forehead. Honestly, I was feeling pretty happy and hopeful a few moments ago.

But then my stream of consciousness flowed in Phoebe's direction. I can't let this afternoon tea go on too long, for fear the dog might have to do her business. The notion of coming home to a wet floor doesn't thrill me much.

And where did my subconscious go as soon as it landed on the dog?

"Things are a little complicated in other areas of my life right now," I have to admit.

What's the point of pretending like everything's okay? She'll only keep asking, and I'll get more and more upset every time I have to tell her things are fine.

"Anything I can help with? You know, for all my years, I do have a few marbles left rolling around in my head."

"If there's ever been an understatement, it's that." I manage a smile, though I'm still feeling slightly miserable. "It's Matt. You remember him, right?"

"Of course. The handsome bachelor at the auction who brought in the most money. Your neighbor. I'm very familiar with him. You bring him up in conversation at least once every time you visit."

"Do I?"

"Like clockwork."

I guess that makes sense. I spend a lot of time with him. "Well, you won't believe what happened yesterday. I can't make any sense out of it myself."

"Can I venture a guess?" When I nod, she continues, "He confessed his feelings for you."

I throw my hands into the air with a gasp. Good

thing I wasn't holding my teacup. "What would even make you say that?"

"Am I wrong?"

"Technically but not exactly. He didn't actually confess with words … he kissed me."

"And?"

"Is this bizarro world? What else needed to happen? He kissed me. Nothing like that has ever happened between us before. It was completely unexpected. I don't know what to do with it."

She lifts a skeptical eyebrow. "Completely? Was it *completely* unexpected?"

"Why do you sound like you don't believe me?"

"Because, I don't."

"I don't know how I feel about that. You think I'm lying?"

"Not deliberately, my dear." She folds her hands in her lap, looking at me straight on. "It's become clear to me that the two of you are quite close. I admit, more than once, I've reminded myself that a caring friend lives across the hall from you, one who happens to be male and in good health. It brings me a measure of comfort to know you aren't entirely alone."

"That's nice." Granted, it doesn't make any sense, but it's nice. I still don't know what any of this has to do with the current situation.

She fills me in quickly enough. "Listening to you talk about him over the past year has made it obvious that the two of you are closer than most friends."

"I've had plenty of close friends in my life," I fib.

"Kitty, it's not nice to lie to your grandmother. But for argument's sake, how many of these close friends were men?"

I wish she wouldn't pierce me with that penetrating stare of hers. There's no way for me to fudge the truth when she looks at me that way. "Not many."

"I would venture to say, none. That's not a criticism, merely a fact. I've never known you to be close friends with another man besides Matt. And I've certainly never seen you smile the way you do when you talk about him. Your voice changes. Sometimes, you bring him into conversation when we aren't talking about anything pertaining to him."

I want to hide in a hole right now. "Is that true? Do I really do that?"

"Fairly regularly, yes." She chuckles at my horror. "It's nothing to be upset about. The two of you are comfortable together, and you like each other very much. What's the harm in that?"

"For one thing, I have never consciously thought about him that way—not since we became friends at least. Before I knew him and he was just a hottie who lived across the hall, that was a different story."

"But now, he's a person."

"A person who routinely criticizes me and teases me and makes fun of me."

"The way a boy does when he has a crush on a girl and doesn't know how to express himself. I believe you told me Bryce did the same thing and admitted his crush on you."

I slump in my chair. Just a little, of course, since I'd get scolded for poor posture otherwise. "Oh, this is killing me."

"Don't take it so hard." She chuckles. "If you're sure there won't be anything between you but friendship, you have to let him know. It's the only fair thing to do."

"I know you're right. I don't have to like it or look forward to it, but I know you're right."

But here's the thing that nags at the back of my mind the entire way back to the apartment, up the stairs, and inside, where Phoebe dances with joy when I come in.

I crouch in front of her, giving her a good scratch behind the ears in greeting.

"Daddy will be home soon. Let's go for one more walk," I coo.

When we're finished, I lead her back to Matt's and get her settled in. "I wish I knew for sure how I felt about your daddy," I whisper before hugging her around the neck and walking out the door to pack for my trip.

Sometimes, I wish life were as simple for humans as it was for dogs.

Chapter Fifteen

"THERE SHE IS!" Paxton greets me with a wide smile and a huge, tight hug when I climb out of the limo he sent to the family's private airstrip.

The family's private airstrip. It doesn't even sound right when I say it in my head.

Dating Blake Marlin was one thing. Yes, he was a billionaire, and yes, his wealth overwhelmed me at times. But he was a little more reserved about it.

Paxton, on the other hand, comes from a dynasty. He might not consider himself pretentious, but they love their money and don't shy away from spending it. I could tell as much on the jet, which included two bedrooms and a dining room.

On a private jet. Which only I was flying on along with the crew, including an attendant who plied me with champagne, fruit, and pastries for brunch. It blew my mind.

"How was your flight?" He leads me away from the limo, where he murmured instructions to the driver.

Apparently, my bags will find their way to my room—I thought we'd be spending the nights together, but he insisted I have my own space to work in.

Because obviously, I'm going to work. This is a once-in-a-lifetime opportunity, and I can't afford to waste it.

"The flight was incredible. You spoiled me with all that champagne."

He chuckles, tipping back the brim of his sexy hat. "You deserve to be spoiled, though that's nothing compared to what I have in store for you this week."

"Oh, really?" My heart skips a beat, I can't lie. Who wouldn't want to be spoiled by him?

"So, what do you think?"

We come to a stop in front of a sprawling mansion. There's a deep porch and rocking chairs and a gorgeous collie currently running down the stairs to greet us. A beautiful black horse is tied off to a post in front, where he nibbles on grass while his tail flicks back and forth.

I would've assumed a house this size would be considered the main house and not a house suited for a single man.

It's like something out of a fantasy. The outside is stone in various shades of brown and tan. A wide path leads from the front door and extends out in both directions and then runs around to the back of the house.

"The pool is back there," Paxton explains. "I hope you brought your suit."

"I did." Meanwhile, I'm counting front-facing windows, and I'm up to seventeen. "How many rooms are there?"

"Six bedrooms, six full baths, plus two partial. Living room, sunroom, office, library. Kitchen, dining room, breakfast room." He scratches his chin. "Oh, and the movie theater and a full gym are in the basement. Does the wine cellar count as a room?"

Right. Because who doesn't need a movie theater in their house? Or a full gym for just one person?

"Wow. This is stunning." And it is. I step inside the airy, bright, welcoming house with its high ceiling and open windows, which allow a breeze to flutter the sheer curtains. "So homey."

"My brother Preston and his wife like that real fancy marble and whatnot." Is it just me, or is he even more Southern now that we're here? It must be a location thing. "I prefer wood, stone, lots of light and air."

He also prefers animal heads on the walls of his study. Welp, I guess I should've expected that. They make my stomach churn a little—these were once living animals. I really can't let myself think of them that way, but it's true—and I tell myself it was the champagne on the jet that's making me feel wonky.

"I can see why you'd rather be here than visiting different offices."

We make a stop in the kitchen, where a pair of women with kind smiles are in the middle of preparing something that smells divine.

"I thought we'd have dinner here tonight, just the two of us," he explains. "Otherwise, we can fly into Dallas or Houston or even Austin, if you want. Except for Thursday night."

"What's Thursday?"

Confusion washes over his face for a second. "The party. Remember?"

Sweat magically makes itself known on the back of my neck. Cold, dread-filled sweat. "No. You never said anything about a party."

"I didn't?" He perches on a stool positioned in front of a wood-topped island. "I could've sworn I mentioned it. Maybe I forgot. It wouldn't be the first time I forgot something."

We're getting off track here.

"What's the party for?"

"It's my father's birthday."

I'm pretty sure I hallucinated that. It can't be true. "Pardon me? Your father's birthday? Is that what you just said?"

"Yeah, that's what I said." He rubs the back of his neck, grinning sheepishly. "Sorry. I must've forgotten to bring it up."

"You certainly did. Is it going to be a big event?"

"I'm afraid so. At the main house and everything." When I very obviously wait for more, eyes wide, he explains, "It makes this place look like a toolshed."

"Fantastic. With all his friends?"

"Only about two hundred."

I'm going to kill him. The man is going to die right here and now, in the middle of this enormous kitchen, with two witnesses. Though they're women and thus probably have more sense than men, so they might understand and in fact back me up and help me bury the body.

Somehow, I manage to keep a non-murderous expression on my face. At least I imagine I do since he doesn't recoil in horror. "I don't think I have anything with me that would be right for an event like this. I'm completely unprepared."

He scoffs gently. "Don't worry about it. We can always go into the city and pick up something for you."

Right, because in his world, things are that simple. In his world, he already knows these people too. He's not going to be an outsider at this party.

He has nothing to prove.

Why do I feel like I have something to prove?

We continue our tour, taking a look at the honest-to-God movie theater he mentioned. There are rows of seats and a big screen stretching along the length of the far wall, even a curtain hanging in front.

"Does this work?" I ask, going over to the old-fashioned popcorn machine.

"Sure. You're free to use it. You're free to use anything in the house whenever you want. I can show you how to set up a movie also. I'm sure there will be times this week when I'm busy with work, so you can do whatever you wish while I'm not here."

"It's tempting. I don't know what my editor would think about it though."

"You can't work nonstop."

"Says you." I poke him in the ribs with a smile. "Right after you got done telling me there's work you have to do this week."

He rolls his eyes with a good-natured chuckle. "Okay, I see what you mean. It's sort of different for me though. I was already away from the ranch and horses all last week, so there are a lot of things I need to catch myself up on. I like to be on top of everything as much as possible."

"The hands-on kind of boss, in other words."

He flashes a wicked grin before pulling me close. "I would rather have my hands on other things. And you're being very generous, describing me that way. Some would say I'm a micromanager, you know."

"If it's your business and your name is on it, why would you not want to be involved?"

"For a city slicker, you understand a lot of things." He kisses my forehead before leading me from the theater room.

A city slicker. Yeah, this party is going to go just great. I know he didn't mean that in any derogatory way, but I'm sure that's the way the people around us are going to see me. The city slicker from New

York, who has never so much as ridden a horse before this week, thinking she can fit into the life of some of the wealthiest people in the entire state of Texas.

I have a feeling I might need to call my grandmother for moral support by the time this is over.

"Come on. We'll ride in my pickup. I wanna show you the horses."

I can't help but smile at the pride in his voice, the excitement. Like a little boy who can't wait to show off his favorite toy.

Only a horse is not a toy. And he is most certainly not a little boy.

Peppermint rides between us, leaning against me and soaking up the attention I give her.

"She's such a sweetheart," I murmur before kissing the top of her head.

"She loves you, for sure. A good judge of character." He scratches her behind the ears. "Do dogs always take to you?"

I have to force my smile to stay put. "Sometimes. There's a dog in my building who I love."

"Oh, of course. The one you were sitting with this weekend." He leaves it there, and I'm happy to do the same.

I first notice a man on horseback inside a ring, watching another man trot a horse around in a circle.

Paxton comes to a stop beside the barn and hops out of the truck. "Come on! Come see."

"Okay, girl," I whisper to Peppermint. "Here we go."

We walk to the edge of the ring, and Paxton introduces me to the man on the horse.

"Sam, this is Kitty. Kitty, this is Sam. He trains our horses."

"Hi, Sam. Nice to meet you."

"Nice to meet you, little lady," Sam says, tipping his hat. He returns his attention back to the ring.

"How's she doing?" Paxton asks.

"Ben has her trotting nicely."

"He sure does. Good progress. I'm going to leave you two to it and show Kitty the rest of the ranch."

"Bye, Sam," I say as Paxton leads me back to his truck.

He drives me around the open land until we come upon a winding river that shines like silver under the cloudless sky. It's breathtaking and so peaceful out here.

"Wow, it's so quiet."

"Yeah, I don't know how you sleep with all that noise in the city."

"Most of the time, I don't even hear it anymore."

"That river separates our land from the next ranch over. I can't wait to take you out on my horse and really show you the land."

Uh, wait, what?

"I believe I mentioned to you that I've never ridden a horse."

"Kitty, trust me, I won't let anything happen to you. Seeing the land on horseback is a whole other experience. Just think how authentic your story will be once you experience it for yourself."

"You really love being out here."

"I do, and between you, me, and Peppermint, I'd rather be out here on the ranch, working with the horses, than sitting in a meeting. And now that you're here, I can think of a few other things I'd rather be doing."

"Maybe it's time you showed me to my room, Mr. Cleary."

"It would be my pleasure, darlin'."

Chapter Sixteen

"THE FIRST THING you need to remember is this: if you're afraid, the animal will pick up on it right away. You have to show them you're the boss. You're the one in charge."

I'm the one in charge? I've never felt less in charge in all my life. Staring up at this gray mare with kind eyes and a gentle demeanor doesn't help me feel better even if the horse seems like a real sweetheart.

"Sadie is the gentlest horse you'll ever meet. I specifically chose her for you because she's so easy to get along with." Paxton pats my shoulder. "You'll be just fine."

"I really wish I had the sort of confidence you do." I manage a shaky smile. "She is a beautiful horse."

"That she is." He looks down at me, tipping my chin upward so our eyes meet. "You know, you don't have to do this. It was just something I thought you would enjoy, but if you're afraid, it would be better for us not to do it at all. You can always ride behind me, if you want. So long as you promise not to squeeze me too tight and break my ribs."

I cast a glance toward Sadie, who clearly couldn't care less either way. "No, I want to do this. I want to say I was able to do this without chickening out."

"Okay, you're the boss."

He shows me how to mount from the horse's left side and then gives me a rundown of how to signal, using my legs and heels. I'm doing my best to keep up with him, but it's not easy. Not when my heart is pounding and my hands are shaking.

But this is fun, right? It's a new experience, one I wouldn't be able to enjoy at home.

That's a bunch of bull. If I really wanted to go horseback riding, I could easily do it in Central Park. There are ways to schedule riding sessions. It's just that riding a horse has never been a priority.

I do want to see his land, however, even though I know I'll never be able to see all of it even if we ride out every day this week.

If I'm being honest with myself, I can admit there's one reason overriding all the others, one singular motivation. Looking confident in front of him. Showing him I'm game for just about anything, that I can handle the things that are important to him.

"You ready?" he asks.

"As I'll ever be."

I'm wearing gloves, so my hands won't slip when I reach up and grab ahold of the pommel. He helps me, hoisting me up, and before I know it, I'm sitting in the saddle. It feels like I'm about a million miles off the ground.

Funny, since Paxton's horse is even taller than mine. The sleek black horse, who now looks eager to get a move on. Paxton has more patience.

"Now, we'll take it slow. When you want to move, press your heels against her flanks. She'll know what to do."

At least one of us will. I do as he said, touching my heels to the horse's sides, and she takes off at a steady walk. Even that seems too fast for me right now, and I can't help but squeal in surprise.

Paxton chuckles. "See? You're a natural."

"You're lying, but thank you."

We share a laugh as he falls in step beside me. We let the horses walk for a while until I feel a little more comfortable before picking up the pace ever so slightly.

"Up ahead, over in that direction, is Preston's house." Paxton points toward the right, where I can just make out a building on the horizon. He then points toward the left. "And that's where my other brother Porter lives with his wife and their twins."

"It really is nice that you all live so close to each other. As an only child, when I was young, I used to dream about having brothers and sisters."

"Meanwhile, I used to sometimes wish I were the only child," he confesses. "It wasn't easy, being the oldest with those two tagging along and making life miserable."

"Isn't that what little brothers are supposed to do? It's, like, their job or something, right?"

"It would seem that way."

"You get along now?"

"For the most part. We all have fairly strong personalities, so it's not always easy. I'm sure if Mama were still around, she would knock our heads together and tan our hides. We would probably even deserve it."

It's clear, the affection in his voice when he speaks of his family. All families have difficulties, I know.

"Do you work together? I mean, like, on the ranch?"

"No. I only train the horses when I have time. The oil is our real business, so most of the time, we're all in the office together." His jaw tightens. He seems to go somewhere else for a minute as he stares off at the horizon.

"I'm sorry," I stammer. "I didn't mean …"

He firmly shakes his head. "No, you don't have anything to apologize for. It's just that we don't share the same ideas when it comes to business. I don't doubt they take their job seriously, and I know they want what's best in the end for the family name. That doesn't mean we agree when it comes to the method of getting where we want to go."

"Where do you want to go?"

This earns me a snicker. "You're very inquisitive today, not that I'm complaining."

My cheeks go red, and it isn't the sun doing it. "Really, if I'm being pushy, tell me to stop asking, and I'll stop."

"I don't want you to stop asking."

I shoot him a look out of the corner of my eye.

"Really." He laughs. "Yes, I suppose it sounds like I don't enjoy talking about these things, but I do. It's just that not many people ever want to know about the things you're asking questions about. They're too busy asking other things."

"Like what?"

"For starters, *why aren't you married with children yet?*" Even if I couldn't see his face, I would know from the sour tone in his voice just how he feels about that. "Don't get me wrong. I like children very much, but I won't marry some woman and bang out a bunch of kids just for the sake of making people happy. They make it sound like it's all about securing the family's future, and maybe it is. But it's also my life. I don't appreciate having my life dictated to me."

"We agree on that," I assure him.

He smiles. "I could guess that on my own, without you telling me."

"Oh, yeah? Am I that easy to read?"

"You do things your own way. Maybe that's part of what attracted me to you in the first place. I admire that."

It's my turn to snicker since I definitely do not feel that way about myself. "What makes you say that?"

"Well, you decided you wanted a certain career, and you went for it. I might not know very much about the publishing world, but I do know it's not usually as simple as writing a book and having it become a best seller. You could've listened to people who told you it was impossible, but you didn't. You went for it anyway."

He has a point, but still.

"Yeah, and I let my editor tell me how to work if I expect to keep that career. I mean, you know the whole story now. Does dating random men for the sake of writing books about them strike you as the actions of someone who's a rugged individualist?"

"I think you're too hard on yourself."

"You can join the club on that one." It's easier to ride when we're having a conversation. I don't have to focus on how nervous it makes me to have hundreds of pounds of horseflesh between my thighs.

"Here's the thing. Now that my father has deemed me worthy of being part of the business end of things, I'm picking up a lot of knowledge. Sometimes, we have to pivot in a direction we didn't foresee in order to keep things on track. Only fools dig their heels in and insist on having everything their way. That's something I'm starting to learn."

From the tone in his voice to the way he almost spits out his words, I'm guessing he doesn't like the lesson.

Which is why I change the subject—and fast. "How many horses do you have? I saw the barn as we were passing by."

His face lights up. Clearly, this is what he would rather talk about. "Aside from the few workhorses and the dozen in training, I have Star here and Sadie. They're just for riding. Sightseeing, getting some fresh air. They already did more than their fair share of work and deserve a nice retirement."

"What do you think, girl? Are you liking your retirement?" I pat her neck. Is that what it's called? I have no idea. Maybe I should've learned a little bit before I flew out here.

In the blink of an eye, everything changes.

Sadie jumps in fear, and I have to hold on with my thighs as tight as I can to keep from getting thrown off her back. I barely have a chance to understand what spooked her before a gunshot cracks through the air, making her jump again and rear up on her hind legs.

This time, I can't hold on. The next thing I know, I'm flat on my back on the ground.

This is it. I'm about to get trampled. Grandmother's warnings race through my head—like, even now, my subconscious can't wait to say it told me so.

Instinct makes me roll to the side, away from the

horses. There's dust in my hair, all over me, and I cough until it hurts. But at least I'm still alive.

"Oh my God, Kitty!" Paxton hovers over me moments later. "Are you okay? Say something."

"Ouch?"

He barks out a laugh while running his hands over me. "Nothing broken."

Thank God for small favors. "What happened?"

He grimaces. "A rattlesnake. But I got it." He pats his hip, where, for the first time, I notice a pistol.

It looks like Texas is even more dangerous than Grandmother anticipated.

The next thing I know, everything goes gray and then dark.

Chapter Seventeen

"I SWEAR, I'M okay!"

Paxton gives me the same look he's been giving me since yesterday afternoon and the whole situation with the snake and me fainting like an idiot. The look of concern.

Ever since then, he's been treating me like something fragile. Like I might break at any moment. I've been pretty much confined to the house, where I woke up from my fainting spell, stretched out across a big, soft bed.

Granted, there's a lot to do in the house, so it's not like I'm being punished or anything.

Yesterday, we watched movies in the theater and ate popcorn and then enjoyed the dinner prepared for us. That was nice and much appreciated since, while I didn't want to worry him, I was hurting all over. Head to toe and everything in between. It isn't every day I'm tossed off a horse's back.

So much for impressing him with my skills and bravery.

"I don't want to leave you alone now. What if

you need help and I'm not here?"

I can only give him a patient smile. "You do remember that you have a staff, right? I've counted at least five people since yesterday. Two cooks, two housekeepers, and a gardener. I think the odds of one of them hearing if I call for help are pretty good. Besides, I doubt I'll need them. I'm just a little sore."

Yes, and the Empire State Building is a little tall. But I'm not going to ruin the time we have together by complaining.

"I won't be long," he promises, pressing a kiss to my forehead and then one against the tip of my nose. "Try to stay out of trouble."

"I'll do my best."

"Oh, I almost forgot." He looks back at me over his shoulder before leaving the bedroom. I can't lie; the sight of him in his jeans and cowboy boots makes my heart go pitter-patter. He's so rugged, so masculine. "I sent out for a handful of dresses to be delivered from a boutique in Dallas. They should arrive sometime today." He says it so casually, like it's the sort of thing people naturally do.

"You sent out for dresses?"

"For the birthday party. You seemed worried about that. I wanted you to feel better. I thought maybe this would be easier, having the dresses come to you since you're feeling poorly. You can try them on here and see which one you like best." He gives me one of his sheepish smiles while I gape at him in surprise. "I hope you don't mind, but I took your size off the tag of a dress you brought with you."

I don't know whether to thank him or roll my eyes with a frustrated sigh. Sure, that was thoughtful, but there are things men don't understand about women's clothes.

Mainly the fact that it doesn't matter what size a woman is. I could choose four dresses by four different designers, all in the same size, and they would all fit differently. Is it fair? No, it's ridiculous. But it's what we deal with.

"That's incredibly sweet. You think of everything."

Yes, that was the right response because, now, he's glowing with pride.

"I just want you to be comfortable and happy while you're here." He leaves the room, calling out, "Stay out of trouble!" on his way down the stairs.

A rather perverse part of me wants to ask exactly what trouble I could get myself into, but it's better to let it go.

Now that I'm alone, I can show how much discomfort, bordering on pain, I'm really in. Getting up from the bed is killer, my stiff muscles crying out in protest at having to move. Demanding to know just who I think I am and whether or not I already forgot what I put them through yesterday.

The deep soaking tub in Paxton's bathroom is the perfect remedy. I fill it with water hot enough to be considered scalding before sliding in and settling back. The water soothes and loosens my bruised, aching body.

So much for the sexathon I was hoping this week would turn into. Maggie will be so disappointed. I certainly wasn't in the mood last night, and unless things improve greatly today, I can't imagine feeling up to it tonight either. That still gives us two more nights before I fly home on Friday.

And then?

That question hangs over me in the otherwise silent bathroom. *What happens after this week? Would I seem hopelessly clingy if I asked that question? Would it turn him off, away from me, if I asked what comes next?*

And what about Thursday? It's not a coincidence, the fact that I had a nightmare about being lost in a huge party full of sneering, cold, nasty people. Nobody would talk to me; everybody kept turning their backs on me. I couldn't find Paxton. I couldn't even find the door to get out.

Gee, I wonder what that dream could have possibly meant. What a mystery.

My skin is pruning by the time I get out of the tub. The soft, fluffy bathrobe comforts me, as does the gently heated bathroom floor. *What would it be like to live in luxury like this all the time? What would it be like to take it completely for granted, the way Paxton seems to?*

Not that I think he's jaded. Far from it. He seems to appreciate what he has, but still, when all a person has ever known is a certain sort of lifestyle, they're bound to lose sight of the big picture. And just how many people don't live this way. This is exactly why my mother wanted me to grow up in Brooklyn.

Not that I have anything to complain about, and I know it.

Darn it. All it took was the briefest thought of my spacious and comfortable apartment, and now, I'm thinking about Matt. Phoebe was waiting for him in his apartment when he got home on Sunday night along with a note, promising she'd been fed and walked at dinnertime. By the time I was up and ready for my flight on Monday morning, I could hear him working away behind his closed door.

I wonder what he's thinking right now. How he's feeling. This time spent apart is a good thing, the timing perfect really. He needs space.

And so do I.

While I won't be getting on horseback again anytime soon, I can at least walk around outside with Peppermint trotting along beside me. It's an absolutely beautiful day, not a cloud in the sky.

The pool is sparkling and inviting and the hot tub along with it. Now, there's an idea. Maybe we can go for a soak tonight, just the two of us, for the sake of loosening my sore muscles. After that, whatever happens, happens …

"I told you, I don't care about that. How many times do I have to say it?" Paxton's voice carries from the barn, a few hundred yards away from the pool.

I can't help but turn in that direction, curious who he's shouting at.

"Shh, it's okay," I whisper to the dog, whose ears went back at the sound of it.

It doesn't take long before I figure out who Paxton's arguing with.

"And how many times do I have to tell you? I don't care whether or not you care. That's just the way it has to be. The sooner you get it through your head, the better."

"I won't let you make those sorts of decisions for me. I'm a grown man, dammit. Just because my brothers—"

"Your brothers know when it's time to stand their ground and time to take a step back and let cooler heads prevail. Last I checked, neither of them is unhappy."

Mr. Cleary's voice isn't the bright, jovial, laughter-infused voice I remember hearing at the ball. He's stern now, strident, maybe even a little cold. Whatever the two of them are arguing about, he's fed up with his son and his opinions.

"You can keep meddling in their lives, but I won't let you meddle in mine. I do as I please. And that's the last I want to hear about it."

When Paxton marches out of the barn, I hurry

out of sight. He practically jumps on Star's back and rides off in a cloud of dust. I watch him until he's not much more than a speck on the horizon.

When I turn my gaze back toward the barn, I find Mr. Cleary watching me from just inside. Most people would flinch or back away if they were caught staring at somebody.

Not this man. He might as well be staring through me.

My stomach drops.

What should I do? Does he know I overheard part of the argument? If so, would he be angry, assuming I eavesdropped on purpose? Should I apologize in advance? What do I have to apologize for?

That would only make me look guilty, and I don't have anything to feel guilty about.

Right?

Chapter Eighteen

THE LACE-COVERED BLACK cocktail dress doesn't exactly fit like a glove, but it's the closest of all dresses Paxton ordered for tonight.

"You look absolutely gorgeous." His hand finds my knee as he drives us from his house to the main house, where his father lives, the house in which he grew up.

"You're sure about that?" I keep smoothing and rearranging the curls hanging over one shoulder. I can't stay still.

"I wouldn't say it if I didn't mean it. You're ravishing. It'll be a miracle if I manage to keep my hands off you for the duration of the party."

I practically have to bite my tongue to keep myself from suggesting we don't go to the party at all. I mean, sex is a pretty good deterrent, right? That might get me out of this.

Something tells me I'm not going to be a welcome guest.

He hasn't had much to say about the fight with his father. By the time he got back on Tuesday afternoon, I decided to gently, casually mention hearing shouting coming from the barn. I didn't mention anything I'd heard, figuring it would be better if he didn't know I'd gotten wind of some of the specifics.

Though I still don't know exactly what it was all about.

"Just another example of how he insists on staying in the past. I swear, it's like he's been asleep the last forty years. This isn't the Dark Ages." That was the most he would give me.

No way was I going to press him for more since the topic so clearly made him unhappy.

So, I suggested a soak in the hot tub, which definitely turned his mood around. It's not like I didn't benefit from it.

And now, I have a hot-tub sex scene to write, so it was a win-win all the way around.

Though I'm sure he wouldn't tell me even if I tortured him for the information, I get the feeling a big part of what they were fighting about was me. *Is it hopelessly deluded of me to think I'm worth fighting about?*

"Do me a favor?" I whisper as we ride over the crest of a hill and an absolute castle appears before us. "Don't let me get lost tonight."

"Don't you worry. I have no intention of letting you out of my sight." His hand creeps up the inside of my thigh, and I squirm a little, giggling. Still, there's no escaping the block of ice now in my stomach.

I've never seen anything like the mansion we're approaching—not in person at least. On TV, sure. This is the sort of insanely sprawling, over-the-top houses the super wealthy call home. There are three wings, extending in a cloverleaf shape around a central structure.

"The center building was built first," Paxton explains, almost like he's reading my mind. "The rest was added on over the years. I love my mama—God rest her soul—but she never knew when enough was enough."

"It's very impressive."

And it is. The long driveway leading up to the circular courtyard is lined on both sides with lit torches casting a warm, almost-magical glow in the otherwise dark night. The sky is so full of stars. The grounds are immaculate, illuminated by carefully hidden spotlights. There are topiaries, luscious roses, towering trees. A pond sits off to one side, complete with a footbridge strung with lights, and to the other side of the mansion sits an array of sparkling luxury cars belonging to the other guests. It's like something out of a fabulous dream.

Or a nightmare. Like the nightmare I had earlier this week about this very party.

Paxton helps me from the car, nodding in greeting to a uniformed valet on our way to the enormous double doors leading inside the house. He places my hand in the crook of his elbow and pats it gently. "Just be yourself. I think you'll be surprised how down-to-earth a lot of these people are."

It's almost adorable of him, the faith he has in me—and in them, for that matter. I wonder if he knows what it feels like to not fit in.

We're greeted by a server upon stepping into the marble-floored entry hall. I accept a glass of champagne with a smile, all the while observing the beauty around me.

I could never get used to the grandeur of my grandmother's home, but this is all a whole other level. A huge stuffed bear sits in one corner of the cavernous study with its paws up, its mouth permanently open in a growl. I wonder if the old man killed it himself and decide it's better to not think about it. I might end up fainting again, and that wouldn't be fun for anyone.

I wouldn't want to be a fainting city slicker who couldn't stand the sight of a taxidermic bear.

There are so many people too. The women are beautiful, dressed to the nines, wearing their jewels and pearls and laughing like they're having the time of their lives. I now wonder if a cocktail dress is suitable for this—Paxton obviously didn't know what to ask for. Only when I see a few women closer to my age, wearing similar dresses, as he leads me from one gigantic room to another do I breathe a little easier.

"Charlotte!" Paxton gestures to a pretty red-head. "Kitty Valentine, this is Charlotte Cleary,

Preston's wife."

"It's so nice to meet you." I take the hand she holds out.

"It sure is nice to meet you," she offers with a wide smile. "We always enjoy meeting Paxton's friends. It's a shame he doesn't bring them around nearly enough."

"As I often remind my sister-in-law, that's because I rarely meet a friend I like enough to bring around in the first place."

"I'm glad I pass muster." I shrug with a smile.

"Bless your heart," Charlotte coos with one more smile before turning to Paxton. "I'm going to find Preston."

"She's real warm, that one," Paxton murmurs sarcastically once she's gone.

"I know what *bless your heart* means," I whisper. "It's not anything nice."

He leans down to kiss my cheek before whispering in my ear, "Don't worry about it. They just want the best for me. I doubt anybody would meet their standards right off the bat."

Is that supposed to make me feel better?

"Paxton! Son, come over here." Mr. Cleary waves him over from where he's standing in front of a fireplace that takes up half the wall and, of course, is decorated with the heads of several species of animals.

Paxton shoots me a concerned look, but I wave it off.

"Go ahead," I encourage, even as I shake inside.

I knew he would have to leave me alone eventually, but this soon? We've only been here maybe twenty minutes.

Standing with Mr. Cleary is another older man, and on his arm is a beautiful girl who can't be much older than me.

And when Paxton approaches, her thoughts are written all over her face.

It would be one thing if her smile hardened. If her eyes narrowed. If she came off as some villainess from a movie of the week. I could hate her or at least pity her for having ideas about him. Clearly, he's in her sights.

But she doesn't look at him like a conquest, like she wants to mount his head above her fireplace.

No. She looks at him with longing. Her breath catches a little. She stands up straighter.

And when I see Mr. Cleary put an arm around Paxton's shoulders and then his other hand on the girl's shoulder, I know exactly what's happening here.

And something tells me I know what they were fighting about the other day too. It was just as much about her as it was about me.

"Don't they look nice together?" I didn't notice Charlotte sneaking up next to me until just now. "They would make beautiful babies, wouldn't they?"

"Yes, I bet they would."

I won't let her get the best of me. I can't. Because she wants me to get upset. She wants me to feel insignificant. I might not have experience here in Texas, but I have all the experience in the world when it comes to catty women who think it's their job to be gatekeepers, to keep outsiders where they belong.

I turn to her with a wide smile. "It's a shame though. Paxton was just telling me the other day how he's not interested in having babies just for the sake of having them."

Her brows come together. "Well, men do say these things, but it isn't always up to them, is it?" She winks like I'm in on the joke with her. "We women have our ways."

Yes, because it's so amusing, tricking a man into being a father when he doesn't really want to be. Meanwhile, Blondie over there is making eyes at Paxton. There is absolutely no way of misinterpreting what she's got in mind. It's pretty obvious from Mr. Cleary's body language and the way he laughs like a Texan Santa Claus that he has something in mind too. He wants this girl to be his daughter-in-law.

"Her daddy owns the second-biggest oil company in the southern half of the country," Charlotte murmurs before slinking off to spread her evil someplace else.

All I can do is watch with a sinking heart as Paxton makes conversation with this girl who is so into him that she's ready to hire a preacher on the spot.

I'm not going to leave. I'm not going to give Charlotte the satisfaction of knowing she drove me out.

I will, however, attempt to find a powder room or someplace else where I can be alone for a minute. All I see around me are curious, scornful eyes. There are more than a few whispers, and the word *northerner* is thrown around as I make my way through the crowd. *How on earth do any of these people know who I am when Paxton has hardly introduced me to any of them?*

Word spreads, and clearly, there's been quite a bit of gossip in the twenty minutes since I arrived.

There's a six-tier birthday cake in the dining room, on a table that looks like it could fit fifty people with no trouble. That's just one of the many things I observe as I search for a powder room, getting more lost all the time.

"Excuse me." I manage to catch the attention of a server, who points me in the right direction. I swear, this place should come with a map upon entry.

Powder room? It's bigger than my bedroom. There's even a sofa in it, one which I take advantage of with a grateful sigh. I'm wearing the same stilettos I wore on our first date, hoping to even out our heights a little, and my feet are already killing me.

What am I even doing here? I could kill Paxton right now for not warning me of this party in advance. I should've stayed at his house for the night, should've pretended to be sick or too sore from the horseback-riding incident.

This isn't my world, and I'll never belong in it. Not that I particularly want to either. But there's something about having those differences and that perceived inadequacy thrown in my face that's particularly painful.

There's a gentle knock on the door.

"Kitty? Are you in there?"

"Yes." I can't pretend to not be here. Not only would that be childish, but it might also take Paxton the rest of the night to find me if he searches every room of the mansion.

"Can I come in? Or are you …"

I can't help but snicker as I get up and unlock the door. "Welcome to my powder room," I murmur before sitting down again.

He crouches in front of me, taking my hands in his. "I was worried when I couldn't find you. Are you okay? There are so many people here. It's a little overwhelming."

It amazes me, the sincerity written all over his face. The concern, the worry. Like he genuinely has no idea.

"No offense, but I had a hard time, watching you and the girl your father wants you to marry standing together like that. Maybe that makes me petty, but I can't help it. It was sort of a slap in the face."

"That isn't what that was about."

"Listen, Charlotte explained it to me. I know that girl is who your father wants you to be with. I overheard enough of your fight the other day to know it's true. And that's fine; he's allowed to feel the way he feels. But you didn't bother bringing me with you when he called for you. You didn't have to leave me behind."

He frowns deeply, searching my face. "You told me to go over to him. You said it was okay."

"Only because I didn't want you to embarrass him. But you didn't have to leave me on my own. You could have brought me to him, introduced me. Something. When Charlotte—"

He rolls his eyes. "Charlotte. She might as well have horns growing out of her head, that one. She's not exactly the sweetest person."

"No kidding. I had no idea."

"She is not the sort of person I want to be with." He kisses the backs of my hands. "Neither is Lana Jones, the girl you saw me with. She means nothing to me. None of these girls do. All they care about is keeping their money in the family, growing their wealth, popping out kids, and bossing their staff around. None of that interests me, and I would hope you knew that by now."

"Paxton, you don't strike me as the sort of person who could be accused of being naive. Don't take it the wrong way, please, but that's how you sound right now."

"Nobody tells me how to live my life. I do what I want. I spend time with who I want to spend time with, who I like. That's all there is to it."

He yanks me closer, one hand to the back of my head. Before I can react, his mouth is on mine, and in his kiss is everything he's been trying to say. He wants me; there's no mistaking that. And right now, it's enough.

"What are you doing?" I whisper at the touch of his free hand on my thigh, moving higher and higher. "Somebody will catch us!"

"I almost wish they would," he growls before scooting me closer to the edge of the sofa, pushing my dress up around my hips.

Yes, there's definitely something to be said for the threat of being discovered.

Chapter Nineteen

"IT'S SO THOUGHTFUL of you to take the time to fly to New York with me. It's nice to not have to fly commercial and have the plane all to ourselves."

Paxton looks over from his seat across from mine. "It's nothing. I want to spend as much time with you as I can."

"I know you're so busy at the office."

"All that matters to me today is being with you. You think it's easy for me, knowing I'm leaving you all alone in the big city?"

"Have you forgotten that I've lived in the big city my entire life?" I give him a teasing smile. "If anything, I was in more danger at the ranch."

He doesn't see the humor in that, his expression turning stony. "You know how terrible I feel about that."

"You have nothing to feel terrible about! Accidents happen. Besides, I still had a lot of fun. I'll have to practice my lasso tricks when I'm stuck on a scene. Usually, I revert to rearranging my books or scrubbing the grout in the bathroom. I need something new to distract me."

He motions for me to join him, pulling me into his lap. "When's the next time you can come out?"

Thank God. I was hoping he would ask me that. "What would be a good time for you? I'll be working all this week, but I might be able to carve some time out of the weekend so long as I'm a good girl and get my pages done."

"Next weekend is your birthday though, isn't it?"

My heart sinks. "Of course. I completely forgot. I'm dreading it because my grandmother wants to throw me a party."

He toys with a strand of my hair. "Why? The way you talked about her, I thought you got along very well."

"Oh, I love her to pieces, but our styles don't exactly match. I told her I don't want one of her big, fancy parties—like the one your father threw the other night. She had a party like that for herself when she turned seventy-five. I always get over-whelmed at those large gatherings."

He wears a thoughtful expression while his hand roams up and down my leg. He promised to take me to dinner tonight, before flying back to Texas, and as such, we're both dressed up. I'm wearing one of the dresses I brought with me while he's in a suit I would love to tear from him with my teeth.

Then again, as we proved in the powder room last night, we don't need to strip naked to have a good time.

I can now check *quickie in the powder room during a fancy birthday party in a mansion* off my bucket list.

"You know, if she's so dead set on having a party for you, it's only because she loves you. She wants to show you how much you mean to her."

"I know," I grumble. "And I know it makes me sound childish."

"No, just determined to have your own way." He nuzzles my neck. "Sounds familiar."

We haven't really talked about what happened last night. About the girl, Lana, and exactly how he plans to ignore his father's wishes.

I did a little digging into the family name on my phone after he fell asleep.

Her father and Paxton's are old friends. And, yes, their company is enormous, spanning not only the southern half of the country, but several South American countries as well.

They're loaded, in other words, and much more the sort of people Mr. Cleary wants his son involved with.

The man didn't even bother acknowledging me the entire night. Message received.

But here's his son, determined to have his way. On one hand, it's flattering. On the other, I feel guilty.

"What's troubling you?" Paxton strokes my cheek with the backs of his fingers, returning me to the present moment.

"The fact that I'm stupid enough to worry about anything else when I'm here with you right now."

He checks his watch. "You think we have enough time to make out for a while before we land?"

"Only one way to find out."

As it turns out, we did, and I even have time to fix my makeup before descending the stairs.

"I have to admit, you spoiled me. I don't know if I'll be able to travel in any other way ever again."

"Good!" He looks very pleased with himself as he helps me into the back of the limousine waiting for us. "You deserve to be spoiled."

"So? Where are we headed?" I have to admit, being back in the city has me feeling more myself. Seeing that familiar skyline out the window as we approach fills my heart with a sense of relief, belonging.

"There's a club overlooking Central Park that I've heard good things about. Do you like jazz?"

"I love it."

"Good. I thought you might like the idea." His phone buzzes, and he looks down at it, smiling at the message. "I think it will be a good time."

Only, when we arrive, the place looks dark.

"You sure it's open?"

"It should be. I made a reservation." He takes my hand, and we walk to the front door together.

"I don't think we should try to go in. Maybe something happened, or maybe somebody got sick."

I might as well not be talking. He opens the door—it's not locked, and that somehow only makes me more nervous.

There are people inside though. I can hear them.

And in another moment, I can see them.

"Surprise!"

The lights go on all at once, and I find myself faced with a roomful of people I know.

"Happy birthday a week early." Paxton hugs me from behind, chuckling in my ear.

I take in the sight of my grandmother, Peter, Hayley, and her sister, Kylie, and her husband, Zack. There's their brother, Brandon, looking like he's ready to party. Even Maggie and Lois are here. Lois looks like she would rather be asleep, but then again, she normally looks like that.

And there's Matt.

My stomach threatens to do a full flip when our eyes meet. He only smiles, applauding like everybody else is.

"I rented out the whole club for the night. It's all about you."

I crane my neck to look up at him, gasping. "Are you serious?"

"And that's not all of it. You'll see." He kisses my cheek before letting me go, so I can hug Grandmother.

"You didn't want me to do something like this, but that doesn't mean I couldn't let someone else do it." She hugs me, patting my back. "Happy birthday, dear."

"I don't know what to think!"

They pretty much pass me around, everybody taking turns to hug me and laugh at how surprised I was.

A single, long table sits close to a dance floor. A live jazz band begins to play soft music while we're served drinks and appetizers from silver trays.

"How did this happen?" I whisper to Hayley once I manage to pull her away from Paxton. I can tell she's slightly smitten with him, much the way Maggie is. My editor is practically salivating.

"Somehow, he got my number. Some people know how to find what they want to find. He asked me to get everybody together."

"Did you try to convince him that I didn't want anything fancy?"

"I didn't want to look ungrateful—and neither should you," she whispers. "By the way, you look awesome. I guess a week on the ranch did wonders for you, huh?"

"Like I didn't tell you I got thrown from a horse."

"Yeah, but it looks as though you bounced back pretty well." She drops a broad wink before going over to hang out with her brother and sister.

Grandmother and Peter are chatting with Lois while Maggie practically hangs off Paxton like a pendant.

I find Matt at the bar, by himself. *Why did he come? He's the last person I would expect to find here. Should I go over and say something? No, that might look a little obvious.*

"Excuse me. I just need to get some air." I give Paxton what I hope is a reassuring smile before stepping out onto the terrace overlooking much of the park.

I wish my heart would stop pounding. The surprise is long over—and really, I should've seen it coming. When he was talking about it on the jet, I should've guessed he had something in mind. But nothing could have prepared me for this.

Dammit, why is Matt here? It's torturous, knowing what I know, knowing he sees Paxton and me together. Maybe I should've tried to talk to him when he got home on Sunday, but I was a coward. It's not like I could've guessed he would end up at my surprise birthday party a week later.

"So, how did the ranch treat you?"

I close my eyes at the sound of Matt's voice. He's standing behind me and off to the side. I can hear the ice rattling in his glass. Well, he didn't confront me; he's not being rude or mean, so I guess I should follow his lead.

"Would it surprise you if I described being thrown from a horse?"

"Not a bit."

"In my defense, there was a rattlesnake, and the horse reared. Paxton shot the snake before it could hurt us or the horses."

"What a hero."

I grit my teeth and shoot him a dirty look. "Could you not tonight? Please? Whatever has to be settled between us can be settled after this."

Matt looks confused. "What needs to be settled between us?"

What am I supposed to do with that? I'm still struggling to formulate a response when he nods, his mouth falling open.

"Oh, that."

"Yes, that. I'm trying to be sensitive to your feelings here."

"Since when?"

"What did I just ask you?"

"Sorry, you're right." He sighs, staring into his glass.

The lights from a dozen buildings around us illuminate his profile. I tell myself not to stare, but I can't help it. Now that he opened the door by kissing me, these thoughts are bound to pop up in my head. Like, what it would be like to wake up next to him in the morning and run my fingers over his scruffy cheek.

He lifts a shoulder, his eyes still downcast. "I was all messed up. I've got to come clean with you and say, I still don't trust him. I'm sorry. I see how much he likes you, but there's more to it than that. He's a complicated person. And I guess, I don't know, I got overly protective. Maybe, deep down inside, I thought I could make you change your mind, make you decide to forget about him. I just don't want you to get hurt."

I try to process this while the rest of the party goes on behind us. I should be in there, shouldn't I? But I can't leave Matt out here either. Not yet.

Especially not when, for some strange reason, his explanation leaves me a little crestfallen. "So, I didn't, like, lead you on in any way?"

"Oh no! No, not at all. I don't want you to think that."

I guess that should make me feel better, shouldn't it? It should come as a relief. So, why don't I feel very relieved?

"I'm glad you're here," I decide to say, and I mean it. "Somebody's got to help me get through being the center of attention."

"There you are!" Paxton joins us—or rather, joins me, wrapping his arms around my waist from behind like he did inside. He's followed by everybody else, all of them arranging themselves on the terrace.

"What's going on?" I ask, a little apprehensive again.

"Watch and see." He points out toward the park. "Just one little birthday present."

Suddenly, the sky is on fire. Red, gold, blue, green. An entire fireworks show just for me.

"I don't believe it!" And I don't, I can't, even though it's right here in front of me.

Everybody oohs and aahs at the right moments. I look around at my grandmother, Peter, my best friend, and her family. I see delight on their faces, and I'm glad.

Only one person doesn't look as impressed.

When the show is over, when everybody files back into the club, where dinner is about to be served, Matt leans in and murmurs just loud enough for me to hear, "Looks like you got your happy ending—finally."

And for some reason, that makes me want to cry.

Chapter Twenty

"THAT WAS ONE hell of a party." Maggie sounds hungover, three days later.

"I have to agree."

"And now that I've met that man of yours in person, I can't help but picture him in all of these spicy scenes you wrote. Did you really fuck in the hot tub?"

I close my eyes and cringe. What would he think if he knew Maggie was talking about him this way? Knowing she was imagining him when she read scenes I'd written between my hero and heroine?

She doesn't let me come up with a response before continuing, "Honestly, you should include a picture of him on the cover. We'd outsell every book you've written so far."

"If you think he's swoonworthy in a suit, you should see him in cowboy boots on horseback."

"No doubt. I can't believe that you didn't take any pictures for me."

"Okay, now, you sound like a stalker."

She chuckles like I'm kidding. "Did you receive the pictures I sent you from your party?"

"I did, and I've already posted a couple of them on social media. Don't worry; I'm not slacking."

"Good. So, you think you'll have the rest of the book finished this week or next?"

"Uh, this week. I know I'm probably jinxing myself by saying this, but this one has gone easier than all the others." I rap my knuckles against the desk, just in case.

"Would it be too clichéd of me to make a comment about things being right?"

"Maybe a little."

"I'm going to say it anyway. That man is clearly crazy about you. You'd better lock this down while you still have a chance."

"You are such a romantic."

"Laugh all you want," she sighs. "What I'm telling you comes from a woman with experience. When you find a man who looks at you the way Paxton Cleary does, you sink your hooks into him, and you don't let go. I mean, the man rented out the entire club for the night. He arranged a fireworks show. He hired professional dancers for entertainment. Top-shelf liquor all night. And the food!"

"It was delicious. I can't imagine how much he must've spent on that."

"He obviously thinks you're worth it—and I don't disagree."

"I'm glad you could be there."

"So am I. Now, get to work, young lady."

"Yes, ma'am."

No sooner do I end the call though than something distracts me. A text message. A text message involving a picture.

A picture of Paxton's bare chest and abs, the frame cutting off just above the happy trail leading further south.

Even this is enough to make me want to fan myself. I can't help but remember the times we've had so far, what his skin tasted like. How it felt to let my fingers trace his muscles.

Naughty boy, I reply. *What are you trying to do? Distract me so I'll never get any work done?*

He replies immediately. *I was hoping you would reciprocate actually.*

My teeth sink into my lip. *What, you want to see a picture of my stomach?*

Maybe something a little further north, if you don't mind much.

The man is like a walking, talking aphrodisiac. I can't help myself. I'm so wrapped up in him, in the excitement of being wanted by him.

Which is why I send him a shot of my cleavage. *Sorry, you're just going to have to fantasize about the rest until we're together again.* I add a bunch of suggestive emojis before sending it over.

No fair. Give a man something to live off of until then.

It's tempting, but I have my limits. I've seen too many people's reputations ruined by sexts to give photos away like they're candy. *You're just going to have to use your imagination. Anticipation makes things so much better later on, don't you think?*

You're killing me—and I love it.

I wish I could stop giggling. I need to get my head in the game, get this book finished.

My characters are reaching their critical moment—when it seems all hope is lost and they can't be together anymore. Only in this case, it's the poor heroine's family and friends who don't think things could ever work out between her and the wealthy cowboy. They don't want to lose her, don't want to see her live a different sort of life that will take her away from them.

And sadly, because she thinks they need her—her parents are still alive but older and somewhat dependent on her—she is willing to give him up even if it means giving up the closest thing she's ever found to happiness.

Cracking my knuckles, I launch into the scene.

"I don't understand this. What are you telling me? We were so happy before, but now …"

She shook her head, fighting back tears. One of them had to be strong, and it was going to have to be her. Because it was for the best. She didn't belong in his world, and he didn't belong in hers. How could she possibly hope to live up to the expectations a member of his world shouldered on a daily basis?

"We both know this can't work permanently. It's time we stop lying to ourselves."

"Why do you keep using the word we, *like any of this is something I want too? Don't I get a say in any of it?" He turned his hat around and around in his hands by the*

brim, curling it up at the edges a little bit and probably
ruining it.

Why that should matter so much to her just then was
a mystery she didn't have time to solve.

"I'm sorry. You have no idea how sorry I am. But
this was never meant to last, right? This was fun, but
that's all it was—fun. We would never make it."

"Says who? I don't feel that way."

He was killing her. Didn't he know he was killing
her? Why did he insist on making this so much harder
than it already was?

"I don't have to like it, but I know it's right. Please, if
you care about me at all, you'll accept this. Our worlds
don't match. There's no way we could be happy in the
long-term."

"To hell with our worlds!" He reached for her, but
she backed away just in time. That was the worst,
watching his face fall as his hands went limp by his sides.
"All I care about is you. I don't care about my family, the
people they know. Honestly, I don't care about the people
you know. I only care about you."

"Here's the thing though. We can't ignore everybody
else in our lives just because we want to. We don't live in
a bubble, no matter how nice of an idea that is. We do
have family. We do have friends. And we can't forget
them. It would make you miserable in the long run—
don't pretend it wouldn't. You love your family even if
they drive you nuts. Just like I love mine."

My phone buzzes, cutting off my next thought. I
usually turn it off or at least put it on Do Not

Disturb during a writing session, but I can't help it. I want to be available when Paxton reaches out. I already miss him, and it's only been three days since the party. He didn't fly out again until Saturday morning, and we spent a mind-blowing night together at The Plaza.

I'm afraid he's become something of an addiction, and I have no plans at the present time to break myself of him.

I'm actually disappointed when I find it is Hayley who texted.

How's it going today? You okay without your big, strong cowboy?

Actually, I text back, *I'm trying to get some work done. But to answer your question, not really. I already can't wait to get back out there.*

She replies with a bunch of laughing emojis. *I never thought you would learn to love the ranch life.*

Yes, because that's what I miss. She knows all too well, and she's only teasing.

It's time for a break anyway, so I get up and stretch the way I try to do at least a couple times an hour. I grab something to drink and some grapes from the fridge.

And then, in a moment of sheer wickedness, I take out the dress I wore to the birthday party for Paxton's dad, which Paxton told me to keep— granted, what would he do with it? It's hanging on the back of my closet door when I take a picture of it and send it to him. No caption. Just a reminder of our exciting little quickie while I was wearing it.

It's not until later, when taking another break, that I wonder why he hasn't gotten back to me. He's busy. I can't expect to monopolize all of his time. I get back to work, trying to throw myself into my writing so when I visit Paxton again, I can do it without a book on the brain.

By eight o'clock, I'm starting to feel little perturbed. Sure, I've gotten a ton of work done today, but Paxton hasn't gotten back to me. Is he pouting because I wouldn't send him anything more revealing than my cleavage? No, he's not some immature, little boy. He wouldn't go off to a corner and pout because I didn't send him a picture of my boobs.

At least, I hope not.

Eventually, I can't take it anymore. I send him a quick text. *How was your day? Hope everything went well. Give me a call if you have the time.*

And then I wait. I clean the bathroom. I clean all the leftovers out of the fridge. I finish unpacking because, yes, I left that to sit all weekend. Packing is so much more fun than unpacking.

Still nothing from him two hours later.

I text Hayley instead, knowing she's busy but needing a little reassurance. *He fell off the face of the earth all of a sudden. I can't get him to message me.*

You're Kitty fucking Valentine. You're fine. He's probably busy, riding horses or something like that.

It makes me laugh anyway. I'm just about to remind her it's pretty late out in Texas when another text comes through, and this time, it's from him. Finally. *Thank God.*

Until I read it.

Dad had a heart attack. In ICU now. Not looking good.

Chapter Twenty-One

"GOD, I FEEL awful."

"He's not out there alone. He has family around him."

I roll my eyes at Hayley's response even though I know it makes sense. But still. "I just remember how I felt when I was going through this with Grandmother. I wouldn't wish it on anybody."

"It's terrible, I know. But remember, you didn't have family to fall back on when your grandmother had her heart attack. Like I said, he does. They all have each other, and that's the way it should be at a time like this."

I pace the living room. Back and forth, back and forth. Chewing my lip, chewing my nails. "I just feel like I should be out there with him."

She's quiet for way too long, which fills me with dread.

"You don't agree with me then."

"I know you want to be with him," she starts, speaking slowly. "And I understand. I really, truly do. I would feel the same way in your position."

"But?"

Her heavy sigh tells me what I need to know before she even elaborates. "But from what you told me over brunch about the way his sister-in-law treated you and the way his father basically ignored you and didn't even bother to acknowledge your presence at the party and how neither of his brothers introduced themselves even though you were with Paxton the entire night and they couldn't have possibly missed you …"

"I get it."

"But do you? Honestly. What do you think it would look like to them if you showed up out of nowhere? This is a time for family, and you might not want to hear this, but no matter how well things are going between you and Paxton, you aren't family. You've only been dating him for a couple of weeks. They would probably see it as an insult."

"I don't care what they think!" The words echo savagely through the air. I didn't mean to shout, but that's how it came out.

At least she manages to keep her cool, which is more than I can say about myself. "I'm sure you don't, and maybe he doesn't either. But if they turn a cold shoulder toward you, what will that do to him? Do you think he needs that right now? He'd not only be dealing with his father in intensive care, but he'd have his brothers and their wives and God only knows who else acting like a bunch of assholes. That won't make anything easier, babe, and you know it."

I let out a tiny whimper before the tears start to flow. "My heart is breaking for him."

"I know, sweetheart. I know. I know you care about him, and you have the biggest heart of anybody I know. That's why he cares about you like he does—because he sees it too. All you can do is promise to be there for him when he needs you. Maybe he'll end up calling in the middle of the night because he needs to hear your voice. Or it might not be until tomorrow or once his father is out of the woods—or if things take a turn for the worse. There's no telling how it's going to go. But he will need you. I know you will be there for him."

"I'll do my best." But that still isn't good enough.

Once I'm off the phone and I finish pacing, I know there's something I need to do. Sitting around has never been my style.

Which is why I get online and start looking for last-minute flights. I could fly into Dallas and rent a car or get an Uber or something to the hospital. It would be an expensive ride, but he's worth it.

I then go to my room and throw some clothes into a bag. I was only able to get a flight in the morning, one that will have me at the airport at six o'clock. Already, I'm spoiled by the whole private-jet thing. It's so much easier to get around when a plane is at a person's disposal.

Then, I send a quick text to Matt, too, though he's only across the hall and I could very easily knock on his door. I'm still feeling a little weird about him though—that *happy ending* comment on Friday night really got under my skin.

What did he mean by that? Was he being sincere? It certainly didn't sound like it. I've been doing this for a year, and for one reason or another, it hasn't worked out. And, now, yes, I think I can finally have my happily ever after with Paxton. I deserve it, and Matt can't take this away from me. And part of happily ever after means taking a last-minute flight to Dallas because the man you've fallen for is going through a brutal time and you want to be there for him.

I'm going out of town again for a couple of days, and I wanted to let you know, so you're not worried if you find me gone. Paxton's father had a heart attack and is in intensive care. I'm flying out first thing in the morning.

And then I figure I'd better get some rest. I'm not used to going to bed this early, but I want to be fully there for him when I arrive. It's not easy, trying to fall asleep with so much on my mind. I can't stop imagining what Paxton is going through, hoping he'll reach out and fill me in as soon as he can.

That's the thing about falling in love with somebody. Their problems become your problems. Their pain becomes yours. And there's nothing you can do to take it away, which is the hardest part of all. It's plain torture, being so far away from him, unable to even hug him and make sure he has what he needs.

I manage to fall into a fitful sleep, waking approximately once every hour and checking my phone for messages. There's nothing from him, which I guess could be considered good news in a way. Things haven't gotten worse, and that's pretty much the best anybody can hope for right now. Amazing how easy it is for me to go right back to that terrible night in December when I got the call about Grandmother's heart attack. I felt so lost, so heartbroken. Like my whole world was turned on end.

I finally get up for good at four thirty and take a quick shower. There's no point in trying to go back to sleep. At least if I get to the airport early, I can grab some coffee and maybe something to read at one of the shops there. I won't feel quite so helpless if I know I'm on my way.

There's a knock on my door as I'm going through everything at the last minute, making sure I have what I need. "Matt, I'm kind of in a hurry." I mean, who else would it be at this time of the morning?

"Kitty? I really need to talk to you."

"Can it wait? Did you get my text?" I wheel my suitcase to the door and then fling the door open without bothering to hide my irritation. "I'm really in a hurry."

For a second, I worry that something terrible happened to him too. He looks stricken, deeply troubled. Almost as bad as I've ever seen him.

"Oh my God, what happened?" I whisper. "Is Phoebe okay?"

"Oh, yeah. No, she's fine. Everything's fine over there." He jerks a thumb in the direction of his apartment.

"Okay, good. So, what's up? I have to get to the airport—"

"Kitty." He holds out his tablet, where he was just looking through news items related to finance. There's a stock ticker running across the top of the browser screen.

And a big, fat headline under that ticker. CLEARY OIL STOCKS STABILIZE AFTER NEWS OF MERGER.

"Okay. What has that got to do with anything?"

"Keep going. Read the rest of it."

"I really don't have time for this," I mutter, but I do as he asked, if only to get him to leave me alone.

I read the first line out loud. *"The sudden death of Cleary Oil patriarch Patrick Cleary comes as a heavy blow to his family—though, if it could be considered one, a silver lining in this situation was the bedside wedding of Cleary Oil heir and eldest son, Paxton, to his longtime girlfriend, Lana Jones."* I gasp in dismay.

There's more, but I can't read. Not only is there no more breath left in my lungs, but the words are also all blurring in front of my eyes.

"I'm so sorry, Kitty. I'm glad I caught you before you went to the airport."

"I don't understand," I whisper. It's like a bomb

just went off in my head.

"If it's any consolation, I'm sure it only had to do with business."

My head snaps up in time with the first tears rolling down my cheeks. "Thank you for the consolation. I have to go now." I close the door before he has a chance to say anything else—like, for instance, that I no longer have anyplace to go.

Chapter Twenty-Two

"HOW COULD I have been so stupid?" How many times have I asked myself that question today? Probably once for every balled-up tissue around me, and there are a lot of tissues.

"I'm so sorry, sweetie." Hayley is whispering, her voice echoing in her office bathroom. She's been calling during bathroom breaks to check on me ever since I sent her an all-caps text not long after Matt's little visit.

"How could I let myself believe he was going to be my happily ever after? The way his dad was yelling at him. The way she looked at him at the party. The way his family basically treated me like dirt—"

"You can't blame yourself," she insists. "I won't say there's a perfectly logical explanation because none of this makes any sense to me either. But I'm sure it had nothing to do with you."

My laughter is a little bitter and certainly humorless. "I'm glad to know the fact that the man I was dating married another woman not three days after the last time we slept together—not to mention the birthday party he threw for me—had nothing to do with me."

"You know what I mean. He wasn't rejecting you."

"Then, what was he doing? This definitely puts a damper on us getting together again, don't you think? God, how could I have fallen for him?"

"I wish so much that there were something I could do. There's nothing so painful as listening to someone you love going through something like this."

All that does is make me cry harder than ever. Wasn't I just thinking that about Paxton before going to sleep last night? Twelve hours ago, I was still under the delusion that there might be a future for us. That my presence at the hospital could grant him a measure of peace.

Dear God, what would've happened if I had shown up at the hospital? How much of a sucker would that have made me? And that nasty Charlotte would've probably taken pleasure in it too. Finally making sure I was put in my place.

"I have to go, but I'll call you back in a little while. Hang in there, okay?"

"I'll do what I can." I drop the phone on the floor next to the couch before curling up in a ball, alternately punching and hugging a pillow, depending on whether I feel angry or sad.

What I didn't tell Hayley, what I couldn't bring myself to mention, is the number of missed calls from none other than Paxton Cleary. He's tried to call me six times this morning alone and sent countless texts, none of which I've read.

He doesn't deserve another minute of my time. That much I'm firm on.

The apartment is so quiet. Eventually, I can't take it anymore, can't listen any longer to the sound of my crying. I put a movie on my laptop and then another, dozing on and off. I wish I could just go to sleep and stay that way, wish I could forget everything for a little while.

Maybe I should order up a whole bunch of alcohol from the store around the corner. Do they deliver in times of crisis? I could look it up, but I don't even have the energy to check. That would require actual effort even if it would only be a little bit.

Around three o'clock, there's a gentle knock at the door. "Could you use a visitor? There's an adorable dog who would like to say hi to you."

I can't see Matt right now. I can't face him. He was right; he was right the whole time. I'm so ashamed.

"Thank you but not right now," I manage in a choked voice since, big surprise, I'm crying all over again.

God, I was so hopeful. Watching those fireworks with Paxton's arms around me, knowing he had gone to all that trouble just for me. What is wrong with him that he would do that? What have I ever done in my life to deserve being led on that way?

I fall asleep again, and this time, when I wake up, it's dark. It makes sense I slept for so long. I'd hardly gotten any sleep last night since I was worried about that no-good piece of nothing. I'm even angry about that—the fact that I wasted sleep over him. Worrying about him, wanting to be with him, wanting to spare him at least a little of the strain I knew he was going through. What a joke. It's like I walked right into a punch, like I left myself wide open to be hurt.

Though this is a little deeper than hurt. This is closer to devastation.

God, I really thought he might be the one. In the middle of the night, back at the ranch, sharing his bed. Watching him sleep, wondering to myself what it would be like to watch him sleep every night. To wake up next to him every morning. To ride at his side—because obviously, in my little fantasy, I would've gotten over my fear of horses.

I allowed myself to think ahead, into the future and what it might hold for us.

And let's not even get started on the nonrefundable plane ticket and how the price was jacked up to high heavens, thanks to the fact that I bought it last minute. Just another stupid thing to add to the list of stupidity I managed.

I'm on my way to the kitchen to open the only bottle of wine in there when there's another knock at the door. "Matt, I'm sorry. I'm not in the mood for company, but I appreciate you stopping by."

"Kitty? I have to talk to you. Please, let me in." The voice on the other side of the door stops me in my tracks.

My stomach churns. I have to hold on to the counter if I have any hope of staying upright.

"Please, Kitty. I can explain. I need to talk to you."

The sound of Paxton's voice makes me see red. *How dare he! Who does he think he is? What is wrong with him?*

"Kitty, please. Give me a few minutes. I came out as soon as I could get away. You wouldn't answer my texts or my calls, so—"

I practically fly to the door on wings of rage and fling it open so hard that it bounces off the wall next to it. "You're a real prince, you know that? Thank you so much for taking the trouble of coming all the way up here. Thank you for breaking my heart in person—oh wait, you didn't. I had to find out on the internet that you'd gotten married overnight."

At least he manages to look embarrassed. I used to think his sheepish expression was cute, but now, I want to slap it off his face.

"I can explain, I swear. It's not a real marriage. I only did it to make my father happy in his final moments."

"Yeah, okay."

"It's the truth. It's all he ever wanted. Yeah, by now, you know he was pushing for me to marry

Lana and merge the companies. I refused. We butted heads over it more times than I could count." His face crumples. "Please. Can I come in at least?"

I drop my shoulders and step aside, so he can come in. It's bad enough that Matt can probably hear every word. He doesn't need to be able to look out the peephole to watch too.

"Thank you." He lingers near the door like he's afraid to come in any further. "I meant every word I just said. I did it for him. My brothers had pressured me into it, too, but I knew it would make him happy. One last thing I could do before he went, so he wouldn't be worried on his way out. He lingered another hour before he died."

The catch in his throat reminds me that, indeed, his father passed away overnight. "I'm sorry about that."

Though honestly, the guy acted like I was lower than dirt, so I hope I'm not supposed to shed a tear over that.

I've shed enough of them to last me quite a while.

"It's been killing me all day, knowing you would probably hear about it somehow. Knowing how hurt you would feel until I explained that it meant nothing."

"You got married."

"For show. I can have it annulled."

"Paxton ..."

"Please, believe me." He takes one step closer to

me and then another. "You're all I want. That hasn't changed."

We both turn at the opening of the door.

Matt lets himself in without knocking. "Okay, buddy, that's enough of your horseshit. You might wanna pack it up and hit the trail."

Paxton's head snaps back. "Excuse me, but this has nothing to do with you."

"You think so?" Matt folds his arms, sneering as he looks Paxton up and down. "Considering I'm the one who's been listening to her crying all day over your sorry ass, I think it has a lot to do with me."

For a second, it looks like Paxton might hit him. I look at Matt, my heart in my throat, wondering if he could handle himself should it come down to that.

After all, I've seen what Paxton is capable of down on the ranch.

Then again, Matt is more than physically capable himself, and he has something else on his side— sheer hatred. It's coming off him in waves, so thick that I'm concerned it will choke me.

"Why'd you come here?" Paxton demands. "I'm having a discussion with Kitty."

"I know. The walls are thin." He shoots a glance my way. "I thought I could offer a little further insight into the situation. Context, you could say."

"Get your sorry ass—"

"No." My voice rings out over Paxton's. "This isn't your apartment, and you don't have a say in who stays and who goes. Matt, let's hear what you have to say."

He looks downright smug, though I can't blame him. Not now.

"Isn't it true that, as soon as word of your father's heart attack spread, your company's stock prices went into a free fall?"

I turn to Paxton, surprised. "Is that true?"

He shrugs. "That's what happens sometimes when things are in flux. There's nothing particularly unusual about that."

Matt nods. "You're right. There's nothing unusual about that. Except we both know that little wedding in the hospital wasn't only for your father's sake. It was for the sake of appearances. You needed some way to assure your shareholders that things were going to stabilize, and what better way to do that than to join your family business with another equally large company? You know, the merger you and your father spent all last week trying to convince the board would be a good idea."

"That was the company you were trying to merge with all along." I cover my eyes with my hands. "Jesus Christ, I'm an idiot. I should've left during your father's party."

"I'm telling you, the marriage doesn't mean anything!"

I drop my hands, which I'd very much like to use around his neck right about now. "Stop lying! You know it means something. And I bet, if I believed you now, you'd string me along for a while. Promising the annulment would come through any day. Swearing you didn't care about Lana, that you had to stabilize the company and keep the shareholders happy. The whole week you were in town, your father bullied you about seeing me, and you spent the whole time pretending like nothing was wrong."

"I didn't want you to know about it because I was trying to work it out!"

I was right about that then. "And when I was there, at the ranch, you fought with him. Your brothers wouldn't even speak to me. Because they knew a wedding was the only way to keep the company together and I wasn't the right girl to marry. They probably bullied you into the wedding at the hospital, and you allowed it! You don't care enough about me to stand up to them, and you know what? That's fine. Business is business. People have married for less. But don't come around me anymore. No calls, no texts, nothing. I want to forget I ever knew you."

"Kitty, please," he whispers, eyes shining like he's on the verge of tears.

This huge man. So strong and virile and masculine.

But such a big, spineless baby.

"Go. Get on your jet and fly away. Have a happy life." I turn my back on him, shaking all over.

He needs to leave now while I can still hold

myself together.

"You heard her," Matt growls. "Out. Now."

"Fuck off," Paxton snarls.

But he leaves, and Matt doesn't.

Not until I need him to.

"Thank you," I whisper, turning my face slightly so I can see him out of the corner of my eye. "I think I need to be alone now."

"Okay. I'm right over here if you need anything."

I manage a small smile. "You've already done so much. I owe you."

"No, you don't." He closes the door with a soft click.

Chapter Twenty-Three

"I CAN'T LIE. This one wasn't so easy to get through."

Maggie clicks her tongue in sympathy. "At least you got through most of it before that snake in the grass showed his true colors."

I love it when she mixes her metaphors. "Yeah, well, I shouldn't have made that comment about everything going easy. It all went to hell right after I said it. Lesson learned."

"Are you okay though? Honestly?"

Honestly? For the better part of a week, I've cried a lot, eaten my weight in ice cream, drunk a lot of wine, and binge-watched two complete TV shows from beginning to end.

But I survived. And I finished my book with a happy ending and everything.

"Yes, I'm okay. Really."

"I'm glad to hear that. I guess looks and money aren't everything."

I can't help but laugh. "You're saying that like it's some great, big discovery."

"Well, I'm sorry you had to go through this.

Take it easy, and I'll be in touch with you soon. We might have to think of a new plan."

"It's okay, Maggie. What doesn't kill you makes you stronger, right?"

"That's what they say. Good-bye, Kitty."

"Bye, Maggie."

It's easier to laugh now too. As soon as I stopped blaming myself for believing Paxton's half-truths and delusions about being his own man, things got a lot better. Sometimes, it simply isn't meant to be.

I got two good weeks out of it. A fireworks show just for me.

And some of the best sex of my life.

Okay, I'm going to miss the sex. A lot.

✧   ✧   ✧

"HONESTLY, I THINK I'm pretty strong for deleting that pic he sent me," I tell Hayley later in the day.

It's my birthday, and as such, we're enjoying our customary drinks and junk food. She even has me wearing a *Birthday Girl* sash.

"If you hadn't done it, I would've done it for you. There are plenty of other fish in the sea." She raises her glass to me. "To you. Best friend, best writer, best person."

"Stop. You're gonna make me burst out crying, and everybody here will think we're two girlfriends in the middle of a fight."

She laughs. "It wouldn't be the craziest thing we've ever done. So, are you getting together with your grandmother later?"

I shake my head. "No, she gave me my gift last weekend at the other party." I hold out my wrist, so she can admire the charm bracelet.

"It's so pretty! Let's see … there's a typewriter here. A book. A little teapot …"

"Since we always have tea together," I explain. "The engraved heart has my parents' initials. And she promised to add more charms over time."

"Beautiful. What a unique idea." She looks up at me with a grin. "So, I have you all to myself this evening, Miss Valentine?"

"Don't tell me you're not too busy to hang out."

"Not too busy for you, babe. I say, we go back to your place, order up a bunch of shit food to go with the shit we've just consumed, drink a bottle of wine apiece, and sing 'Happy Birthday' at the top of our lungs."

"That's the best idea you've ever had."

We hurry to finish up and half-drunkenly giggle the entire way back to my building.

It's a beautiful April day. Warm, sunny, with the promise of summer on the horizon.

I love my life. I really do. It's days like this, birthday aside, that drive it home. I have terrific friends. I live in the best city in the entire world. I love my job.

Life could be a hell of a lot worse.

For starters, I don't have to marry someone I don't want to.

"What's this?" I stop in front of my door when I notice the door leading up to the roof is standing open.

"Hmm. Probably nothing. Maybe Matt went up there and forgot to close it behind him." She nudges me. "Hey, you wanna invite him to join us? It might look weird if we're hanging out and being obnoxious and he can hear everything from next door."

"Eh, he's getting his social life back on track. He's been out the past few nights. I doubt he'd want to waste time with us."

"Even better. He'll probably turn us down, so no harm done. Come on!" She starts for the stairs, running up before I can catch her.

"Slow down! You know I can't—"

"Surprise!" Hayley jumps up and down, clapping. "Gotcha!"

Yeah, she got me. So did Matt. And everybody else on the roof—Grandmother, Peter, Hayley's family.

"What is this?" I don't know what to look at first. The lights strung up over the roof. The birthday cake sitting on a table near the roof's ledge. The chairs set up around it.

Matt's smile is wide. "This is what we were originally going to do for you, but ..."

My eyes fill with tears. "You planned this for me?"

"It's not an entire jazz club, and the music will come from my phone, but yeah."

It's the best thing I could have imagined. So much better than what Paxton planned. Sure, that was nice, but anybody can throw money around. This took real work from my friends.

And my grandmother.

I give her a hug before shaking a finger in her face. "Now, what business do you have, walking up six flights of stairs before climbing up to the roof? With your heart problems?"

Peter chuckles. "Don't worry. It wasn't that bad."

Grandmother sneaks a glance over at Matt, who's setting up the music. "He carried me the entire way to your floor."

I don't know what surprises me more. The fact that he carried her or the fact that she allowed it.

"I know." Peter laughs before giving me a hug. "I was as stunned as you are. Happy birthday, sweetheart."

"Thank you so much." My head is spinning. I don't know which end is up.

Matt knew how much it would mean to me, having her here. So, he made it happen.

It doesn't take long for the dancing to start up. Matt's playlist is fun, made up of music from the '50s and '60s.

"Come on," he urges my grandmother, holding a hand out. "I promise I'll take it easy on you."

Kylie joins me in watching them dance, grinning from ear to ear. "Wanna know a secret?"

I gasp. "You're pregnant?"

"No! Good Lord, girl. Do I look pregnant or something?"

"Sorry, sorry. I was already three drinks in when I got here, and now, I'm on number four." I hold up the beer from the cooler beside me. "What's up?"

"You look much happier and more relaxed than you did at the other party. Like you actually want to be here."

"Because I actually do. This is much more my speed."

And now that the sun is setting, the lights criss-crossing overhead look downright magical. Everybody's happy, smiling, having fun together. A slower song plays while Hayley is dancing with Zack so Brandon takes Kylie's hand to lead her to the dance area. When Peter steps in to dance with Grandmother, Matt concedes which leaves just the two of us without partners.

"It only makes sense, Valentine." He holds out a hand. "Come on. I get one dance with the birthday girl."

It's strange to be this close to him, to be so aware of him. I know it would be entirely wrong for me to get all caught up in feelings for him, especially right now.

It would also be entirely too easy, what with me

being on the rebound and everything.

Which is why I have to keep a cool head and my hormones in check. Though the drinks flowing through my system aren't helping either of those things.

"Thank you for this," I whisper, looking around. Grandmother looks so happy, so at peace. "Thank you for making sure she could make it up here too."

"Oh, she told you about that?"

"Please. You should've known I would pounce on her for walking up all those stairs."

"She put up with letting me carry her so long as it meant being here for you. This was something we all wanted for you."

"I couldn't love it more. I mean that." I look up at him, his face all aglow from the twinkle lights, and damn, it's hard to keep a cool head.

Why have I ignored the feelings he stirs up in me for so long? Am I that dense? Or just stubborn?

"I'm glad. I'm glad you can have a nice birthday party on your actual birthday. I'm glad you know how many people love you."

My breath catches even though I know he means it as a friend.

Doesn't he?

Good thing the song ends when it does and turns into something more upbeat because another ten seconds and I might've kissed him. And I've already seen the damage that can do.

Though really, considering the man put together

a surprise party with my best friend, there couldn't be too much damage.

Just the same, I catch his hand and hold him in place for another moment. "You know how you said I had my happy ending?"

He winces. "I wish you wouldn't remind me. That was low."

"No, it wasn't. You were right." I take another look around. "This is it. This is my happily ever after. And if this is the best life has to offer, I'll take it. Because this might be the happiest night I've ever had."

"I hope you mean that." His fingers close around mine. "I really do."

"Come on!" Hayley waves us over. "It's time to light the candles and tear into this cake."

Matt grins down at me, pulling me toward the table with the cake, where Zack and Brandon are lighting the candles. "Do you know what you're going to wish for?"

Yes, I think I do.

ABOUT THE AUTHOR

Jillian Dodd is the *USA Today* best-selling author of more than thirty novels.

She writes fun romances with characters her readers fall in love with—from the boy next door in the *That Boy* trilogy to the daughter of a famous actress in *The Keatyn Chronicles* to a spy who might save the world in the *Spy Girl* series.

She adores writing big fat happily ever afters, wears a lot of pink, buys too many shoes, loves to travel, and is distracted by anything covered in glitter.